THE IRON TRACKS

Badenheim 1939

The Age of Wonders

Tzili: The Story of a Life

The Retreat

To the Land of the Cattails

The Immortal Bartfuss

For Every Sin

The Healer

Katerina

Unto the Soul

Beyond Despair:
Three Lectures and a Conversation with Philip Roth

The Iron Tracks

The Conversion

THE
Iron Tracks

Aharon Appelfeld

TRANSLATED FROM
THE HEBREW BY
JEFFREY M. GREEN

SCHOCKEN BOOKS
NEW YORK

Originally published in Israel as *Mesilat Barzel* by
Maxwell-Macmillan-Keter Publishing House, Jerusalem Ltd.,
in 1991. Copyright © 1991 Maxwell-Macmillan-Keter Publishing
House, Jerusalem Ltd. This translation was originally published in
hardcover by Schocken Books Inc., New York, in 1998.

Library of Congress Cataloging-in-Publication Data
Appelfeld, Aron.
[Mesilat barzel. English]
The iron tracks / Aharon Appelfeld ; translated from the Hebrew by
Jeffrey M. Green.
p.   cm.
ISBN 0-8052-1099-7
I. Green, Yaacov Jeffrey.   II. Title.
892.4'36—dc21   PJ5054.A755M4713   1998   97-27982

Random House Web Address: http://www.randomhouse.com

Book design by Maura Fadden Rosenthal

THE IRON TRACKS

CHAPTER

1

Since the end of the war, I have been on this line, as they say: a long, twisted line stretching from Naples to the cold north, a line of locals, trams, taxis, and carriages. The seasons shift before my eyes like an illusion. I have learned this route with my body. Now I know every hostel and every inn, every restaurant and buffet, the vehicles that bring you to the remotest corners. I can sit in a buffet and imagine, for instance, what's happening in distant

Hansen, how the snow is falling there and softly covering the narrow lanes. Or Café Anton, where they serve warm rolls in the earliest hours of the morning, with coffee and cherry jam. In these godforsaken places such pleasures beckon me, exciting my memory for days on end. I have long since learned that in the end, thoughts, however noble, vanish like the wind, but fresh rolls, homemade jam, not to mention a cigarette, have a taste that stays with you for days. Often just the thought of Café Anton is enough to drive a pack of evil thoughts from my mind. I love those tiny, remote places. Large cities, I avoid like the plague. They fill me with dread. More grievously, with melancholy.

Others may possess spacious houses, shops, even warehouses. I have an entire continent. I'm at home in every abandoned corner. I know places you won't find on any map, places with a solitary house, a single tree. When I first began to travel, I would get lost, confused, stuck. Today with one telephone call I'm out of the maze. I'm familiar with every kind of rural transportation, which drivers work on Sundays and holidays, who is prepared to risk a snowstorm, and who is hopelessly lazy. In short, who is a friend and who is not.

In marvelous little Herben, about which I shall have more to say later, my regular driver Marcello awaits me on April fifth. When I see him from the train window, happiness rushes through me, as if I were returning to my lost hometown. He has been waiting for me on that date for more than twenty years. While I am still standing in the carriage door, he rushes toward me, takes the valise from my hand, and ushers me into his cab. From little Herben we drive to a place called Upper Herben, a two-and-a-half-hour trip. During the drive he tells me everything that has happened in Herben, about himself and his friends, and of course his ex-wife, who has been squeezing alimony out of him for years. Thus it is every year. And in this repetition lies a strange hopefulness. As if our end were not extinction but a sort of constant renewal.

The trains make me free. Without them, what would I be in this world? An insect, a mindless clerk, or, at best, a shopkeeper, a kind of human snail, getting up early, working eight or nine hours, and in the evening, with the remains of his strength, locking up and going home to what? A disgruntled wife, an overgrown, ungrateful son, a stack of bills. I detest those somber places called houses. I board the train, and instantly I'm borne aloft on the wings of the wind.

A train is by nature heavy, even clumsy. But in open spaces, when it gains speed, it transforms itself, defies gravity, and soars. At night that soaring has a special quality. You sleep differently. During the first years that ride would make me dizzy, give me palpitations. To-day I board the train like a man on his way home. If the dining car is comfortable, I sit there, and if not, I find a window seat. Empty cars amuse me. The thought that I'm alone in a car oddly pleases me. I maintain one rule: no sandwiches and no thermos. A person sitting on a train, nibbling a sandwich and drinking from the lid of a thermos, is lower in my eyes than a beggar. I'm willing to spend five American dollars for a cup of coffee, on condition that it is served to me. Simply being served a cup of coffee staves off my depression for a whole hour.

Another matter, the music. In recent years they've installed loudspeakers in the dining cars. I love music, but it must be soft. I loathe drums. They drive me mad. In my youth I fled from classical music as from funerals, but gradually I learned to appreciate it. It's a subtle potion. Once you submit to it, you can't live without it. After an hour of string quartets I'm a new man. The music soothes my nerves, and I respond, if I may say so, quietly and without self-pity.

When I enter the dining car, I listen to what the loudspeakers are playing and check to see who the waiter is and who the other diners are. A coarse-looking waiter is likely to drive me from the car, but if his face is kind, I try to win him over. I slip him a bill or two, and he turns off the drums and puts on a classical station. The old-timers recognize me. They know they'll be rewarded.

THE IRON TRACKS

A heated railroad car with good music is better than any hotel room. Hotels spread melancholy and despair. Not so trains. They can intoxicate every one of your senses to the fullest. To be honest, my competitors, my enemies, also infest the trains and force me to maintain great vigilance. My competitors are short, thin men whose quickness is not that of youth, but of those who fear for their lives. They are terrified by the open platform. They see me, and in a flash they take cover under awnings and disappear onto the first train. Like me, they're experienced creatures of the tracks.

Often I'm tempted to approach them and tell them that I, at any rate, have no interest in this rivalry. For my part, I am prepared for any compromise, for any division of territory. On one condition: no further competition and no animosity. I said I am prepared to compromise, but in fact I have done little to raise the subject with them. Years ago I bumped into one of them in the dark and said, in our language, "Why do you run away from me? What harm have I ever done you?" He was so startled that he went pale and said nothing. Since then I haven't exchanged a word with any of them. I do know one thing: they are not many. Six or seven in all, and they apparently follow the same circular route that I do. Once I found one of them in an empty car. He was curled up in his coat and clutched his narrow valise with both hands as if holding a sleeping infant. I wanted to wake him and invite him for coffee, but I thought better of it. You must not rouse a man from his slumber.

True, from time to time, I am oppressed by sudden fear, inexplicable revulsion. These moods, or whatever you want to call them, used to paralyze me. More than once I have locked myself away in a remote hotel because life suddenly seemed dark and without purpose. The winter in these regions is gray and long, and in the morning it is too depressing to get up. Once I spent two weeks in bed because it seemed to me that a new war had begun. A confession: I like to sleep during the day better than at night. The thought that the world is frantically going about its business while I doze in a big bed, wrapped in three soft blankets, is charged with a hint of revenge.

Over the years I've learned to master some of my fears. Today I get up and without hesitation step over to the sink and begin to shave. Shaving, I have learned, is an activity that arouses optimism. Time at the sink restores the desire for travel and the memory of gliding on wheels. The minute I step onto a train, my life opens up, I walk upon solid ground.

Were it not for my work, I would never leave the confines of the stations. Everything is available on the train: excellent music, glorious views, and, on occasion, a woman. There is nothing like love on a train. Sometimes it lasts only a station or two. The main thing is that you'll never see the woman again. Of course, sometimes you get entangled, and you suddenly have, aside from your valise, a sluggish creature who keeps demanding coffee and cigarettes. Thus I repeat to myself: love for two stations and no more. Fleeting loves are beneficial and never painful. Love for a station or two is love without pretense and soon forgotten. Any contact beyond that pollutes the emotions and threatens to leave behind recriminations. Women, I regret to say, don't understand this. They do themselves a disservice, and me too, of course.

I said love of this kind is soon forgotten, but I take that back. My memory is my downfall. It is a sealed well that doesn't lose a drop, to use an old expression. Nothing can deplete it. My memory is a powerful machine that stores and constantly discharges lost years and faces. In the past I believed that travel would blunt my memory; I was wrong. Over the years, I must admit, it has only grown stronger. Were it not for my memory, my life would be different—better, I assume. My memory fills me up until I choke on a stream of daydreams. They overflow into my sleep. My memory is rooted in every one of my limbs: any injury strengthens the flow. But in recent years I have learned to overcome this. A glass of cognac, for instance, separates me from my memory for a while. I feel relief as if after a terrible toothache.

CHAPTER

2

It has been forty years since I first harnessed myself to those racehorses known as trains. Were it not for my weariness and certain women, I would never leave the confines of the stations, which I've also learned to love. There are stations where you find excellent sandwiches, superb coffee, and even a moment of true rest. Crowded platforms sometimes give way to silence, but often, I must admit, my stations are crammed with rushing people, and baggage, and the smell of chemical fertilizers. You would be better off standing outside and waiting for the next train.

My annual route is circular. Actually oval. It begins in the spring, rounds off, and finishes at winter's end. It's a route with endless stations, but for me there are only twenty-two. The rest are of no consequence. I know my stations like the palm of my hand. I can reach them with my eyes closed. Years ago a night train skipped one of my stops, and my body stirred at once. I trust my body more than my mind. It detects the error on the spot.

Every March twenty-seventh I take the morning train from Wirblbahn and begin my journey. I prefer the morning train to the afternoon express. Express trains make me dizzy even now. The night before my departure I stay awake and stand by the window, awaiting the verdict. If the sky is clear, I know that this year my travels will go as planned, and people will be friendly. But if the sky is low and dark, it is clear to me that the year will be a mess, thugs will harass me, and my profits will be small.

I hate superstitions, but what can I do? In recent years they've clung to me like leeches. I live by signs, by codes whose meaning I alone know. It is hard for me to justify this, but the truth cannot be denied: certain people arouse within me the will for life and joy, and others, often unintentionally, grind me into the dust. A taxi driver who tells me, "I knew you'd arrive today, so I refused a fare and waited for you," revives me instantly. True, taxi drivers are fond of me, because I give them something extra, but not only because of that. Sometimes they sit in the buffet with me for a good hour, recalling what I told them during my past visits, and laughing at all the new anecdotes. In their hearts they know: I belong to their tribe of poor souls.

At seven in the morning I am ready with my valise at the Wirblbahn station. Every time I leave this place or return, anxiety seizes me. My legs weaken, and pressure builds in my gut. Only two tranquilizers can subdue such an attack. Because of this anxiety, and for other reasons, I have sought to change the starting point of my journey. Until now I've been unable to do so. I will explain: in flat Wirblbahn, which is nothing more than a row of warehouses, a few watchmen's huts, and a wretched inn, in this accursed place, my life ended and I was reborn. The Germans brought our train to this remote station and left us here. For three days we had been bolted inside. On the third day, the train stopped moving. The wings of death had departed, but we didn't know it. We were already captive to visions of death. The next morning someone released the bolt, and a stream of light washed over us. That was our return to life. I still feel the light

on my body. As of that morning my strange new life began. Sometimes it seems that everything springs from
that morning. Neither death nor rebirth is glorious. That
morning the people were not joyful. They remained where
they were.

For me Wirblbahn is a mute chapter. A believer
makes his lips speak in any situation. But paralysis grips
me every time I remember that return to life. We were
twenty-four in all, a few dead people, and two children,
in whose eyes the light had dulled. They sat in the doorway of the railroad car. Their legs dangled, and they
asked for nothing. The plain was broad and looked, for
some reason, like a giant rectangle that had been divided
into large squares. The spaces between the square shapes
were empty, barren, for everything that grew had been
cut down. Here, it turned out, stood the warehouses where
we were going to work.

A man touched my arm and said, "This is not
bad, but too late." He immediately returned to the railroad car. I remember his face and the sound of his steps.
His steps are still with me, so that sometimes I imagine
hearing them even as I am embraced by a good woman.
Wirblbahn is a wound that won't heal. I sense it especially
on hot summer nights, a wound that lurks in secret and
suddenly flares up. I was certain that it was my dormant
ulcer, but in recent years I've discovered that the memory

of Wirblbahn is what causes this pain in my stomach to gather strength. Oddly, this only happens to me in the summer and only at night. Once I manage to drive the sight of Wirblbahn out of my head, the pain stops.

Nevertheless, I am compelled to return here every year. I stay in the inn for two weeks, and on March twenty-seventh, I set out. If I found someone here it would be easier for me. But there's scarcely a living soul. The few guards are asleep or drunk, the owner of the inn is deaf. During the war he fought on the Eastern Front. That is where he lost his hearing. He is not ashamed. He hangs pictures of himself at the entrance. He was a platoon sergeant.

A few years ago I saw a man loitering in the court-yard of the inn, and I was certain I was seeing one of my rivals, someone who had come back to life here like me. That was of course an illusion. No one returns here, just me and the shadows I bring with me. Here desolation reigns forever. What am I doing here? I keep asking myself. That's how it is every year.

Last year I couldn't restrain myself and wrote a note to the innkeeper: "Where were you during the war?"

"I got as far as Stalingrad," he answered in his clear hand.

"And there you lost your hearing?"
"Indeed."

"Hitler deceived the world," I wrote.

"Not true," he replied without hesitation.

"Why?"

"Hitler wanted to destroy the Jews, and indeed he destroyed them," he explained.

When I didn't answer, he added in big letters: "It was a great mission, and it succeeded."

"But they still exist," I couldn't refrain from writing to him.

"A mistake," he didn't hesitate to reply.

Once he revealed his hidden desire to me, I ought to have killed him. There is nothing simpler than killing a man, and yet for some reason, I cannot do it.

The moment the wheels roll out of the station, I swear to myself I will never return here, but my vows are empty. My route is fixed, more fixed every year. Imprinted on my body, it cannot be shaken.

The trip north from Wirblbahn isn't difficult, maybe because of the music. Fine music intoxicates me more than fine cognac. Happily, on this stretch of the route there's no need to bribe the waiter. Like me, he too likes string quartets. If there's no one in the dining car, we sit together and get drunk on the music. His name is August, and he is five years older than me. He surely took part in the war, but I don't dare ask him where. Hatred of the Jews here is fierce, and after two or three drinks, it is given voice. I have found sensitive people here, dedicated to classical music, who don't hesitate to declare their hostility to the Jews.

The minute I leave the confines of Wirblbahn, the pressure eases, and I feel relief. Not complete relief. Two weeks in Wirblbahn leave their mark. It is hard to extract those geometric forms from your mind. They etch themselves within you with all their angles. To be honest, I only free myself from the sights of Wirblbahn in little Herben. There a hot bath awaits me. I soak for three full hours. Hot baths have the power to draw me out of melancholy. Not every bath, of course. Remote hotels are likely to have cramped bathtubs, and others, just showers. A sweaty body is preferable to an irritating shower. Only in little Herben have I found a bathtub that suits my body. Only there do I grant it a bit of rest.

CHAPTER

3

After three hours of steady travel the train stops at
Prachthof, a little village that sits on a green plateau. In
this village lived my former sweetheart, Bella. I haven't
seen her for years, but she lives within me, a mute and
constant presence. No day passes without her. I know the
station in Prachthof like my own hand. I used to return
here as a dog returns to his kennel. I often wish to get off

and linger here, if only in the buffet, but I restrain myself and remain in my seat. Fortunately, the wait is short, and I close my eyes and get through it. The excitement is the same. The years, you see, have not done what they are supposed to do.

I met Bella after the war in a warehouse, not far from Wirblbahn. She was nineteen, a mute flower adrift in a polluted sea. No one knew what to do with the life that had been saved. People shamelessly hoarded supplies. There were bitter quarrels. Life was violent and ugly. The camps shadowed us everywhere, as if we had not yet left the cages of death. I took Bella's hand and pulled her outside. She was pretty, the kind of beauty that seems to flourish only in the barren reaches between the living and the dead. We ran away to the mountains. For many days we walked in the tall grass without exchanging a word. The summer spread over the lush meadows, and we would sleep for hours in the fields. Eventually we arrived in Prachthof, a small village with a dreary center. The houses were made of local stone. "Let's stay here," I said, so we stayed. I had a few dollars that I'd gotten from the Joint, and two watches. Death, which had followed us all the way, released us only in Prachthof.

The next day, saying nothing, she collapsed into sleep. At first it seemed like ordinary sleep, but two days later it became clear that this was different, a kind of sinking. I was frightened and tried to rouse her. She would wake up and rise to her feet, utter a few syllables, and with a smile such as I'd never seen in my life, she would once again collapse. I considered leaving her and heading north, as everyone was doing, but something within me, perhaps fear, wouldn't let me, and I stayed with her. I didn't stay willingly. Pity is not a pure virtue.

After two weeks of sleep, she awakened. Sleep had wrought changes in her face. She was starved, as after an illness.

"What happened to you, Bella?" I asked.

"Nothing."

"Why did you sleep so much?"

She bent her head and said nothing.

"Where were you?" I asked.

She looked at me, and I saw the abyss yawning in her face. That short, gaunt creature, who from close up had looked like a destitute refugee, was now taller than I. She seemed to say, Why are you bothering me? Sleep is my language, and I have no other.

Nevertheless, my tongue goaded me, and I asked, "What did you dream?" Again she looked at me with that mute gaze, and I knew I had been heartless.

The secret lodged itself more deeply within her. Her face blossomed, and a crushed smile clung to her lips. Her gaunt beauty receded.

"How do you feel?" I tried again to make her speak.

"Fine."

"What language did you speak at home?"

"Yiddish."

"Have you forgotten it?"

"No."

That was all I managed to get out of her. Her replies were one word, sometimes a single syllable, as if her tongue had been cut out. It was spring and I was reminded of another spring. The long war years had erased scenes of home from my mind. The others sat by campfires warming their hands.

Meanwhile, I ran out of money. What I had to sell, I sold. Refugees flooded the place on all sides. They bought and sold and fondled each other in the empty warehouses. "Bella," I tried to rouse her from her muteness. "We don't have a penny, and we have to get moving." She didn't seem to understand or didn't want to be a burden, so I left her and joined the smugglers. Whoever wanted to live joined the smugglers. They breathed life into dry bones. Among them were tall, thin men, who carried bundles on their shoulders with ease, like fishermen. There were pharmacists, a veterinarian, delicate people who before the war sat at carved desks and wrote prescriptions or memoranda. But by the platforms they seemed like the rest of us—criminals.

Smuggling intoxicated us. We smuggled cigarettes, lighters, cameras, watches, cognac, what have you. It was a broad network that stretched from Naples to Copenhagen, active people who stirred up the region and brought the police to their feet. Luckily for us, everyone was tired, the officials were confused, and a little bribery bought them off.

Occasionally I would return to Prachthof. Bella continued to change. The creases vanished from her forehead, and a kind of rosiness permeated.

"How are things?" I would begin by asking.

"Everything's okay."

The secret in her face was still hidden. She was working in the kitchen at the Joint. People handed her bowls, and she filled them with soup. If there were potatoes or rice, she would serve them with the same gestures of forbearance, as if she worked without benefit to herself.

"Join me," I urged her.

"And who will work in the kitchen?" she answered simply.

Every time I returned to Prachthof, we would sit together in silence. It was hard for me to talk to her. The words clung to my palate, and what came from my mouth sounded crude and insulting. She grew taller and cast a frightening spell around her. Finally, I stopped coming back. Now I realize that no woman has ever known my soul as she has. Since then I've had many women, some of them attractive, but only with Bella did I know true silence. Today I know there is much pretense in talk. Only a quiet person earns my faith.

In time I heard she married a refugee who had gotten rich, and they had two children who went into their father's business. That is what the rumors said. Forty years have passed since I last saw her, but the hidden pull toward her has not ceased within me. Sometimes I imagine, but surely I am mistaken, that she also thinks of me.

4

From Prachthof I continue north. The train passes through rural stations without stopping. Thank God nothing ties me to them. I sit in the dining car and drink coffee. I bribe the waiter with a small sum, and he imme-diately turns on the classical station. Even now it's hard for me to remove the image of Bella's face from my mind. Over the years she's matured within me, her face has thinned, her hair has grayed, but the muteness of her eyes has remained. Once a fellow refugee told me that he had seen her in a dry goods store, measuring out cloth for a customer. "Did she ask about me?" "She asked," he answered. Since then she has breathed within me more intensely. In my mind she no longer feeds refugees in the Joint kitchen but measures out cloth in a store. Her husband stands at the cash register and takes in the money. The boys have gotten fat from too much idleness. But Bella doesn't scold them. She watches them out of the corner of her eye, and when they catch her at it, they get annoyed and rudely chide her.

Until five years ago I kept up this relentless pace, but since my ulcer was discovered, movement has become difficult for me. After a day of travel I need rest. I calm my stomach with light foods, have sworn off fried meat, and eat a lot of yogurt. But I won't give up smoking. Without cigarettes I'm not a man. My hands shake, my memory falters. I've told the doctor, and I say it again here: I won't give up cigarettes. If there's any point to getting up in the morning, it's knowing that a cigarette awaits me on my table. Without cigarettes, what would be the reason to get up? If a woman scolds me for smoking in bed, I get rid of her.

I worked as a smuggler for three years. Three years of constant coming and going, danger and fear. We forgot ourselves in all that activity. No one asked why, when, or how. As if we were trying to accomplish just one thing: to loot every warehouse. What we didn't do during the years of the war, we did now: we moved rapidly. In three years, I amassed a considerable sum. If I'd invested the money wisely, I would be a rich man today.

Then suddenly I ran out of energy. I would sleep for days on end, wake up and stand by the window. Emptiness seeped into me down to my toes. Had it not been for nightmares, I doubt I would have moved. They were my hidden taskmaster, driving me from place to place. I would board a train, travel for three or four stations, and change hotels. Hotel rooms didn't make sleeping easier. Sleep in a hotel is either light or frighteningly deep. I didn't return to Bella. I was afraid of her muteness. It seemed that madness was trapped within her. I'd rather crawl through stations and keep changing hotels than return to her.

In an inn a refugee approached me, a tall man with old-fashioned elegance. "I know you, comrade," he said. When I told him my family name a smile spread over his lips, which conveyed his connection to me. Later, in the buffet, he told me he was about to head south to reorganize the cells that had been destroyed.

"Anyone still alive?" I asked, full of dread.

"Just a few, but loyal."

The word "loyal" was whispered among the secret circles that my father had been involved with. "He's loyal," Father would say, meaning that the man had been a Communist since youth, that he'd taken part in open and clandestine operations, that he'd served time in prison, and also that he'd proven that his loyalty was unswerving. My father had been a Communist since youth and had eked out his days organizing meetings and strikes far from home. He was hardly ever with us. My mother became bitter and took solace in drink. I would often find her sitting in an armchair, muttering to herself. She worked as a secretary in a small textile factory, and with great difficulty supported the household. Father would appear like a gust of wind and then disappear. Their life together was not happy.

Rollman, it appears, had known my father well. He too, like my father, had been one of the great organizers of the party. Jewish Communists have a particular kind of face. Their restrained voice indicates powerful will, and they always wear short leather jackets. Another sign: most of them are bald.

That evening Rollman spoke at length and with enthusiasm about our duty to rebuild, adopt orphans, exorcise ghosts, and plant faith in people's hearts for a better life. Later, his visionary gaze changed, and he said abruptly, "We have been ordered to send the refugees back to the East. Palestine is an illusion and a disaster."

"How will this be done?"

"With song. You have to close the ranks with song."

From childhood I had known the power of song over the masses. My father used to take me to workers' meetings, where they would sing folk songs, hymns, even snatches of operas. In time Father left the Jewish camp and went over to the Ruthenian neighborhoods, where they didn't sing at meetings but roared. Father would say that the Ruthenians were good and talented people, that exploitation had corrupted them, and as soon as the yoke was removed from their necks, they too would become engineers and doctors.

The next morning we took the first train out to the refugees. They were encamped on a long beach crammed with people and shacks. Rollman immediately found an empty spot, a few meters of canvas, and some crates. A Communist from youth knows how to set up a stage.

Rollman appeared that very evening. He sang in a low voice, as if talking to himself. The multitude of refugees, with burning candles in their hands, surrounded the small stage and responded by singing the chorus. The songs grew more powerful, and gradually they began to sound like prayers.

After the performance, a refugee harshly attacked him. "I'll never forgive you," he shouted. "I remember your speeches in Lvov. The Communists cannot be forgiven. They must be condemned everywhere."

Rollman composed himself. He stood there and bent his head. The man didn't stop berating him. He spoke of the commissars who had seduced the young with false promises, causing misery to old parents, and the strikes that had been catastrophic for small Jewish businesses.

The next day, too, Rollman's performance was impressive. He sang folk songs and workers' songs, and songs that brought to mind ancient prayers. No one interfered. After the performance there was a great silence. I remembered my mother, who had also been a Communist from her youth. It was said that she had taken part in the murder of General Porotzky, the chief of the secret services, who had viciously persecuted the Communists. The years, solitude, and bitterness had removed her from active duty. Increasingly, she withdrew into herself.

Later it got hot, and the mood on the beach became volatile. The Italian police would arrest people and confiscate their goods. Short men would race after them with bribes. Life at the beach was full of such hustle and bustle. Whoever was capable of striking would strike. No one ever said, "Enough," or "Silence." A tall woman was there, with wild hair, who spoke Lithuanian Yiddish. After every one of Rollman's performances she would rush into his arms and say, "You've given us back our home, comrade." But not everyone agreed. Some bitter people would stretch out their arms and shout, "Strangle the Communists, death to the thieves!"

These threats did not deter Rollman. The humid-
ity would sometimes muffle his voice, but he didn't give
up his performances. A refugee, one of the gaunt ones,
begged him, "Why don't you go farther south? The refugees there are quieter. Here there's violence and much
hatred." Clearly, the man was concerned about him and
wished to save him from his enemies. Rollman ignored
these pleas. Old Communists are used to insults. They
love torment. It strengthens the will and also one's ca-
pacity for suffering.

After the performance he would return to the
tent, drink five or six cups of tea, and fall asleep. He slept
most of the morning. His sleep, like his being, was a
mixture of practicality and secrecy. When he sang, his
face would fill with emotion, like the High Priest's in
the Temple. But in the tent, near the crates, he was like a
craftsman who knew the power of restraint. He ate mod-
erately. During the time I spent with him, he revealed
many things to me, including something my father had
hidden from me: the death of Uncle Moses. Uncle Moses
was Father's younger brother, a Communist from youth
and a district chairman. At the time of the persecutions,
he was murdered in his hiding place. I had known his
death hadn't been easy. Now I heard about the murder for
the first time.

One evening everyone was preoccupied, people
were dancing the hora in the open area, buying sand-

wiches and lemonade at the improvised buffet. While everyone was saying "good evening," a refugee stepped up to Rollman and said, "The Jewish Communists deceived Jewish youth. They wrested them from their parents, put them in squalid cells, and in the end, sent them to Russia, right into the lion's mouth. We won't forgive them. They have forgiveness neither in this world nor in the next." The words rushed out as if from a memorized speech. Then, without warning, he drew a pistol from his coat pocket and shot Rollman in the head.

People were stunned. No one moved. Before long the full extent of the horror was clear. Rollman lay in a pool of blood. The murderer, a short, thin Jew wearing a cap, stood next to his victim and muttered, "The Communists destroyed the Jewish people."

"Why have you done this?" shouted a refugee.

"You don't know?" answered the murderer.

Soon Italian guards came and handcuffed the murderer. He went off without a word. A restrained excitement was in his face.

Right after Rollman's murder, I boarded a train and fled north. The sharp pain came later, many kilometers from the scene of the crime. I am a creature of the tracks. Every time the whip lands on my back, I board a train and flee. Only a railroad car with its rhythmic vibration has the power to soothe me and put me to sleep.

What would I do without that somnolent rhythm?

True, a drink and a few cigarettes can banish fear from my heart for a short while, but only the train, it alone, can tranquilize me completely.

After the murder I traveled for many days. In a moment of weakness I almost got off at Prachthof. But as soon as I stood up and reached for my valise, Bella's mute face rose up before me. I don't know if she was already married then. In any event, I did not get off. I closed my eyes and kept them shut until I felt the whirl of the wheels beneath me.

Since then my days have glided over the rails with a kind of haste, as if they weren't days, but the gathering darkness of twilight. It was a profound sleep, sometimes disturbed by the pounding of hammers. I hate those vigilant inspectors who strike the wheels and send evil sounds out into the night. Were it not for those dusky inspectors, were it not for their chilling sounds, I would be another man.

On that long journey the course of my life was composed. I learned to live at a distance from people, suspiciously. I confess, I have no faith in anyone outside the train. They repel me. Over the years, I've found a few friends who remain faithful and wait for me, a few women. Hotels are usually good to me, and there are a few inns whose silence I've learned to respect, and sometimes, a window bids me welcome.

CHAPTER

5

When did I first come to Herben? It's safe to assume I was probably tired, dizzy, and tormented by nightmares. I do remember this: I didn't expect to find anything at that desolate, wretched station. But what a miracle, in that very place, the Lord granted me two gifts: the driver Marcello, who awaits my arrival each year, and the perfect bath at the inn of Upper Herben.

THE IRON TRACKS

When the train stops, Marcello leaves his cab and rushes toward me, grabs my valise, and seats me at his side. The encounter, which takes place once a year, on April fifth at 3:30 P.M., always moves me. This Italian in exile, in whose company I dwell for two or three hours, grants me, without knowing it, the feeling of home. It was as if I had returned to my native city. We sit in the buffet, exchange impressions, and eat sandwiches. The place isn't elegant, the music is harsh, but the meeting is heartening, and the coffee is good and strong.

For years he's been struggling with his ex-wife, who is extorting alimony from him. I know the story in detail. Nothing new has happened for years. A court session, postponed once, was postponed again or if it took place, it was interrupted because the witnesses didn't appear. Still, it seems to me that Marcello is telling me his most precious secrets. For his part Marcello remembers everything I have ever told him. I haven't much news either, but he's glad for any scrap and hopes that one day I will join him so that we can establish a taxi company together.

Later we drive to Upper Herben. There, in the modest inn, the bath awaits me. The owner of the inn, a pleasant old Frenchwoman from Alsace, tastefully dressed, announces that my room has been prepared. Let it be plainly said, the room is nothing special. But more than once the bath adjoining it has restored me to life. I'll never forget it.

I got to Herben a few months after Rollman's murder. After his death I was afraid of everyone, even myself. The train carried me, but not at the desired speed. Finally, I arrived in Herben. Marcello said, "They have a bathtub you'll be pleased with," as if he knew my hidden needs. I thought he was fooling me. Before long I discovered he was speaking the truth: the bathtub wasn't large or splendid. Its sides were covered with blue tile, not rounded, and the surface wasn't smooth. But, to my astonishment, it suited the contours of my body. Flaws may abound in it, but for me it's a shelter. When I first sank into it, my eyes brightened. Since then, every year, I renew myself in it.

Only after the bath did I sense the presence of time in my body. It wasn't happiness, but a kind of relief after a prolonged illness. A memory dormant in my limbs stirred, and I saw the forests of Vatra Dorna, where my mother took me when I was five. We walked and picked mushrooms beneath the tall trees. It was autumn and the sun was low. The forest was bathed in a golden light.

In Herben that memory returned to me, and since then it hasn't stopped flowing. I didn't know what had been hidden within me. I was fifteen when I was separated from my father and mother. I was certain that my life in Slavic lands was over. From then on I would wander and be borne from place to place. In Italy I'd be Italian, and if I went north toward Austria, there I would be at home. My mother had imparted the German language to me with all its subtleties in poetry and prose. Her loyalty to that language was no less than her loyalty to Communism. At night, before going to sleep, she would read me poems by Heine. I doubt that I understood anything. But the sounds flowed softly into my ears. I would be cut loose from the waking world and slip into deep sleep. Even in difficult times, when she grew morose, swallowing drink after drink, she would pick up a book and read, like someone preparing for better times.

She was killing herself day by day in her room, and I didn't know it.

"Why didn't you go out and buy me some cigarettes?" she would ask.

I would be taken aback. "You didn't ask me to, Mother."

"I'm sorry. Please do me a favor and go buy me a pack," she would say, handing me a bill. I was afraid to leave her alone.

You must get used to living without me. I have to go somewhere else, her eyes would tell me.

Where is that other place you're going to? my eyes would ask again and again.

What does it matter? her eyes would reply wearily, ending the exchange.

In the last year we spent together she stopped reading to herself and to me. Once a week her friend Mina would come to her, and they would sit by the window. I didn't understand their conversations, perhaps because they were often silent. Mina was her friend from childhood, and she remained loyal to my mother. Other friends had distanced themselves, because she was a Communist, and because of the rumor that she'd taken part in the murder of the chief of the secret services. She never spoke to me about that murder. Surprisingly, all of this comes back to me in Upper Herben.

After Rollman's death my body shrank as during the war. I went from train to train, seldom stayed in hotels, and lived off my savings. I was certain that when I used up the dollars that were sewn in the lining of my coat, my life would end.

I only stay in Herben for one day. Once, in the past, I was exhausted when I got there, and wanted to stay over for another day. That was a mistake, though not one I will ever repeat. For hours memory flooded into my head, as if seeking to drown me. My distant childhood, lost sights, appeared before me like a melting sea of ice. Since then I no longer overstay. I spend just one day in Herben and no more.

CHAPTER

6

Yesterday I turned fifty-five. I spent the day by myself on the local between Hofbaden and Salzstein. The train is always empty on that stretch. For a bribe of three schillings the waiter turned to the classical station, and I sat alone in the dining car while Brahms sonatas washed over me. Once, the years passed as though on their own. Then, on my fiftieth birthday, I felt a sudden pinch in my heart, and I knew immediately that those were the years accumulating within me. Since then I count them. I know this counting is pointless, and it would be better to refrain, but what can I do? On April thirtieth the pinch in my chest reminds me that a year has passed, and once again I stand in the place where I was. The distances that I have traveled have worked no wonders. Barring disaster, I'll be on the same train in another year. I'm not complaining. I have learned to appreciate the small things that come my way. There are days when I leave the train drunk with visions and sights, walk into the hotel, and fall fast asleep, as if after a day of real exertion.

In Salzstein I am a welcome guest. The owner of the buffet in the station, Gizi, a converted Jew, is glad to meet me. We have an unspoken secret that binds us. Once he whispered in my ear a word in our language. Since then we've been friends—soul mates, I would say.

He prepares two sandwiches and some borscht for me and tells me a little about the goings-on of the year. Two of my enemies were in there drinking coffee. They too, it seems, have become weary. One of them has decided to emigrate to America. In the depths of my heart I hope that one day they'll all clear out and leave me alone. True, their malice isn't evident, and perhaps they don't intend to harm me, but the thought that they are scurrying about the same way I do is enough to drive me mad.

As for Gizi, he has managed to do what I will never be able to do. He has changed. He looks like an Austrian in every respect, even his hair. Apparently, it's due to his wife, with whom he lived for several years. Now they are separated and waging a mighty battle over their property. The struggle with her has become his life. She, of course, stops at nothing, as they say. When they separated she told everyone his true identity, and since then people have been conspiring against him. But he stands firm—always giving back as good as he gets.

Strangely, a couple of hours in his company restore my will to live. Perhaps because of his candor. Once he told me: "I converted because I loved my wife and because she saved me during the war. For six years I went to church with her, but in the seventh year I couldn't any more. My knees felt weak. I asked her to remove the icons from the house, but she refused. Since then I've been sleeping in my buffet. I have a folding cot, and I sleep on it. I left her everything, but she also wants this station, which I built with my own hands. These planks are mine, and I'll defend them with my life."

"Aren't you afraid of hooligans?"

"They don't frighten me," he said with a crude gesture that shocked me.

The short time I spend in his company leaves his features engraved in my mind. At times it's hard for me to understand him. Once he said to me, "Then I had to convert to Christianity, but now I don't have to do this any more. Now the time has come to love plainly and to look straight into the eyes of the living and the dead." I was about to ask, What do you mean? But I didn't ask. I have learned that answers clarify nothing.

From here I continue on to Upper Salzstein, a little village nestled in the forest. There, in a small cabin hidden away, lives Comrade Stark. Right after the war he arrived here, bought the cabin for nothing, and fixed it up. Since then he hasn't budged. But don't worry, he's not cut off from the world. From here he sends out his articles, pronouncements, and amplifications. He stays in contact with the comrades, and the survivors, who will rebuild the movement.

Before the war, Stark was one of the well-known secretaries of the movement, but since then he's been both leader and aide. He writes the letters and he mails them. Here the scattered few gather to celebrate anniversaries, commemorate the dead, and sit together over a drink. Once people spoke of sending Stark to the Soviet Union at the head of a delegation to gain recognition and funds, but for some reason, the plan was never carried out. That didn't make him less loyal. On May Day we, the dispersed, gather here, some by train and some on foot, not more than ten. For a moment we bring to life what was and is no more.

Stark has aged. But on May Day he swallows two or three drinks, girds his loins, and goes forth to wrestle with ghosts and melancholy. He used to speak a lot about the future, about change and conquest. Now he speaks of the glories of the past, of the leaders who sacrificed their souls for their faith.

Several years ago in Stark's cabin I met Jacob Kron, a childhood friend of my father's. Together they spent more than a few years in prison. He told me that Father was once unanimously chosen by the Ruthenians to be their secretary and to lead their strikes. But at the last minute someone remembered that Father was a Jew, and pointed out that it wasn't right for a Jew to lead Ruthenians. Father didn't lose faith. He never returned to his origins, the Jewish quarter. Instead he remained loyal to the Ruthenians, speaking in their behalf and organizing their mass meetings. He outwitted the police and performed his service in poverty and devotion. Kron had also known my mother well. He called her a revolutionary in heart and soul, someone who did more for the revolution than any other comrade. He, of course, was referring to the famous assassination in which my mother took part.

Two days in Stark's company restore a whole world to me. I sink into it as if into a drugged slumber. These aren't easy times. Stark is moody. By turns, he chides and consoles, and when faith is rekindled in him,

his face changes, he stands taller, and youth blooms
again in his eyes.

Once Mina would fill the evenings with folk
songs. For hours she would fan the fires of memory with
her voice. In recent years she hasn't been seen. Five
years ago she married an Italian and moved to a remote
village. The village, it seems, did not bring her peace. She
dreamed about soil and the simple life, and she found
liquor and sloth. At first she struggled against these
vices, but she soon learned that the Italian village was
deeply rooted in its traditions. The party headquarters
was just a tavern where the men would gather for amuse-
ment at night. The lectures and discussions were of little
interest, and if you couldn't accept things as they were,
in the end the village would expel you. And that is how it
was with her. Since then she's been shunted from place
to place, and she avoids even her friends. At the time
Stark made great efforts to bring her back. Those efforts
brought nothing. She became one of the shadows that in-
habit railway stations, slipping away whenever an eye lit
on her. Here she is remembered fondly and her memory
is evoked as if she had passed away. A year ago Stark declared, "My heart tells me that next year Mina will return
to us. I miss her melodies. They are like fresh air."

Last year no one came to him. Even the few, the
faithful, have stopped sending him money for subscrip-

tions to the party journal. But Stark is not one to sit idle. Besides the reproachful letters he sent to his associates, he prepared a pamphlet for better days. Now he is working on his masterpiece, "The War Against Melancholy." That book, he believes, will bring people out of hiding. "Melancholy is a thrashing serpent," he writes. "It must be fought to the death."

I know what he means. I have witnessed its attack on my body. When melancholy grips me, I lose the power to move even a single meter. Once, in a small railway station, it gripped me in my sleep, and in the morning I couldn't shake myself loose. Were it not for the owner, a kind old Italian woman, I would have remained stuck there for who knows how long. Since then I have been careful. As soon as I sense it approaching, I take out my bottle and fight back. Stark has gathered a lot of material from ancient and modern sources on this affliction, and now he'll sit down and put them all together. I eagerly await his book.

I spent two days with Stark. He spoke for hours and kept silent for hours. On the second day, seeing that I was packing my valise, he raised his eyes to me and asked, "Where are you going?" His gaze was full of sadness, as if he had also seen in me his lost son.

"I have obligations," I said, so as not to give in to my feelings.

"Tell me," he asked softly.

"I'm tracking down the murderer Nachtigel," I said in a voice not my own.

"That's a great mission. You must cling to it with all your might." He spoke to me the way he once must have spoken to his subordinates.

Thus it was, every year. But this year the parting was different.

I handed him a fifty-dollar bill and said, "Here's my contribution to the place."

"It's too much," he said.

"I made money this year. I have more than enough."

"And what about the future?" he asked in a fatherly voice. His look shrouded me in silence for a moment. I saw how his broad shoulders had shrunk, how sorrow had made his brow pale. Why can't we pray? I wanted to cry out, but I immediately realize how foolish that would have been. He showed me out, and I knew that this meeting was our last. If we saw one another again, it would not be in this world.

CHAPTER

7

I make my way north from Salzstein on a local. In this
season the fields demand a lot of work, and passengers
are few. The whole train is mine, and I settle in next to
the window. In the first years after the war, people would
gather from all over and stay in Stark's cabin. There were
about ten of us. We would spread out blankets and sing
throughout the night with Mina. Stark would rise to his
feet and inspire us with his conviction. As always, of

course, there were those of little faith and a few scoffers. They hadn't the power to put out the fire.

The thought that this modest assembly too will break up, and that I will soon pass through Salzstein as I would other anonymous stations, terrifies me. In Salzstein the gates of memory open before me, leading me back to my father and mother, and I enter, without hindrance, to the party headquarters and secretaries' offices, but most especially the prisons, where the comrades refined their faith and learned to be wholeheartedly devoted. Now I, too, deserted Stark. He sat all alone in his cabin, launching angry letters. With his own hand he cut himself off from the few who held him in esteem.

As the train advances, I feel the searing inside my body. At first Stark's cabin was a sanctuary, full of inner joy, but in recent years, every word wounded and every grimace stung. The pain, as always, would come later, when you didn't expect it. After Salzstein it is hard for me to fall back to sleep. I am restless, tossing and turning. In the past I would stop in little Lenzen, have a few drinks, and go on, but Lenzen is no longer what it was. The station has gotten dingier, the buffet is like a cavern. I prefer being jostled on the train to stopping in a neglected place. Such a station dismays me, a burden my body must bear.

If nightmares interrupt my sleep, I stop off for a day or two in Gruenfeld. That's a little village with a dairy and an inn. The inn isn't fancy, but surprisingly it has the power to put my nightmares to rest. My nightmares, if I am permitted to speak of them, are neither fleeting nor few. They are always abundant, and only certain places and particular foods have the power to quiet them.

In Gruenfeld they serve me borscht, black bread, and fresh milk and cheese. These miraculously draw me out of the mud. Fresh dairy products, I have learned, are better than medicine. But the best can be found only here. The cheeses that I buy in grocery stores aren't fresh. Cheese that's not fresh, like stale bread, destroys my appetite. For days afterward I touch only coffee.

I could stay on, but the people here are rude. Since they discovered that I'm a Jew, they treat me with obvious coolness. But I don't care. Better a little scorn than a long nightmare.

I once found an old man here who proudly told me that his paternal grandmother had been Jewish. This stain had prevented him from being accepted in the military academy. During the war he had been sent to the Eastern Front, and from there he had returned as an invalid. He spoke of his stain the way he spoke of his wound, without resentment. He worked in the courtyard of the dairy, and when he sat down on the bench sorrow flowed directly from his blue eyes. I enjoyed his company, his silence, the way he broke his bread. That stranger, who didn't like me much, would give me confidence. Once I told him that my stay with Stark had saddened me, and it was hard for me to sleep. He didn't answer me. He just watched me as if to say, I understand you, but what was necessary should not be condemned. I am grateful to him for that glance. A glance is sometimes stronger than a word. It can revitalize you. Three years ago he died. Since then Gruenfeld has changed for me. I don't linger there more than a day, or I skip it entirely.

From Gruenfeld I continue north. This is a land of forests and lakes that conjures up the image of my native city, which is buried within me. If I have a grasp of anything on this earth, it is of my lost hometown. Rather: that neglected little house on Siebenbirgerstrasse, where I would return to see my mother. Sometimes it seems that all my travels are to that place.

My mother spoke little, but the few words that came from her mouth filled my heart. In time the patience vanished from her eyes, and sharpness settled in. I didn't know yet all the ups and downs of her life, but I sensed that I should be near her. She would sit in the corner of the room, imprisoned within herself.

"Mother."

"What?"

"Why won't you talk?"

"What?"

Thus the words would echo through the dark room. There were days when I was afraid of her silence. I would open the door and sit down right there. The light would flood the hallway, and birds would come and peck at grains of wheat in the palm of my hand. In winter I would press close to the window and watch the sleds skimming over the snowbanks. At night she would cover me with three blue blankets. Sometimes a surge of affection would burst from within her, and she would hold me softly. Then, too, she spoke little, her words sounding as if she was forcing herself to overcome her silence. As if freeing herself from her own prison.

Later she shut herself off even more. Her face had closed, and her lips twitched. Sometimes I would find her leaning on her arms, supporting her thin body as if afraid it would collapse. Her shoulders shrank, like someone trying to become as small as possible.

Without realizing it, I was handed over to my father's custody. He would drag me from meeting to meeting and from gathering to gathering. My father was completely immersed in the task of liberating the Ruthenians, and I became a kind of appendage to his mission. More than once I was forgotten on a bench and would fall fast asleep. At night he would carry me on his shoulders to the cabin where he slept. That's how I learned the Ruthenian language. My father had kept me away from his mother and father so that I would also learn the ways of the Ruthenians. He was convinced that their way of life was correct and organic, and were it not for the estate owners and the Jewish merchants, they would live in complete harmony with nature.

At the age of six I spoke Ruthenian like a native. My father was proud of that. The language of the Jews repelled him. He used to say it exuded the odor of grocery stores and sounded like the rustle of money. Nor did he care for German. He used to say that in Czernowitz the Jewish merchants wore their shabby German like borrowed finery. Sometimes he would go way into the mountains, to the remote cells of the party, to members mainly housed in abandoned apartments or stinking stables. My father's appearance would change there. He would be like an estate owner dispensing favors in every direction. The simple Ruthenians liked him and would serve him deep bowls of sour cream and goat cheese. Sometimes he would forget me in a hut or absent-mindedly leave me behind. For hours I would sit and gaze at the evening lights and at the animals slowly returning from pasture. If there is one vision deepest in my heart, it is of a Ruthenian village at dusk. At night my father would remember me and shout, "Erwin, Erwin."

At the age of six I returned to my mother. During the year I hadn't seen her, she had changed greatly. Her dresses had grown longer and more faded. Her face was gaunt, and her knuckles stuck out. She looked at me for a while and said, "Do you remember me?"

"Mother!" I ran to her.

Still, it wasn't like before. The school was far from the house, and every morning she would take me to the brick building. I didn't inherit my parents' courage. My Ruthenian classmates frightened me. Often I would stand next to the wall and tremble with fear.

"Why are you afraid, my dear?" my mother would ask softly.

"They scare me."

"They won't do anything to you. They're children like you."

During our year apart her face had sealed entirely, and she barely left the house. Sometimes one of her friends would come and sit with her in silence.

A year later I was returned to my father. My mother walked me to the gate of the house, and, without exchanging a word with my father, put me in his care.

CHAPTER

8

The train advances, and now it's close to the little village of Gruenwald. In the past I would get off here and stop for a day or two. A Jewish couple lives in the village, refugees without children. I met them a few years after the war, and afterward I used to return and stay with them. They were friendly and hospitable. They had a long sleeping porch where they put up guests. In the evenings we would sit at the table and drink tea. They quietly bore the suf-

fering of the camps within themselves, without unnecessary words and without slogans. He was about forty, she
a bit younger. Because of their generous nature, people
would call at their house, stay for a day or two, and pass
on. They owned a grocery store with a housewares sec-
tion. He was called Mark, she, Rosa. One evening, when I
told them my name, they turned pale and silent. That sudden, sharp muteness afflicted me: I spoke with fervor, in
words that weren't my own, about my father and mother,
who had suffered for the common good all their lives. My
words did not soothe them. In fact, it was evident that the
sound of my father's name scalded them.

That night I packed my valise and left without a
word. In the empty station two drunks sprawled. They
jeered at me and barked like dogs. I could have struck
them, but as a rule I never hit people. Now, when the
train stops in Gruenwald, I stay in my seat. From the window I can see that the grocery store has expanded. Customers stand by the shelves and at the cash register. The
owners have certainly forgotten me, but I shall not forget the evenings I spent in their home. They left their
scars.

Now the train rises toward the thick forests of
Gruenwald. Even in May the light does not come through.
The train speeds into a tunnel of green, and the smell
of moss returns me to a childhood home, this time to
Grandfather's dairy cellar.

During the summer, when I was in my mother's care she would send me by wagon to her native village, to her father and mother. She herself did not go back there. It was a small village surrounded by tall trees, and from a distance Grandfather's low house resembled an abandoned kennel in the heart of the forest. That, of course, was just the way it looked. Inside the house were two long rooms, and attached to the house was a shed where Grandfather would sit most of the day with his books. He was the village rabbi, and toward evening many people would gather at his doorstep. They were tall, bearded Jews. The smell of horses wafted from their long garments, and whips never left their hands. The women were also tall and sturdy. They sat in covered wagons and nursed their babies. The children beneath the wagons looked like Gypsies. They ran about barefoot.

The people would arrive toward evening. The neighing of the horses and the ringing of the bells would put an end to the silence. The men would get down from the wagons first and stand there, hesitant and confused. Then they would head for the entrance. Near the door they paused awkwardly. Grandmother would come out and speak to them softly, and they would return to their wagons.

For hours I would sit and observe their waiting, which would continue until dark. I saw the women kneel and whimper beside their wagons, which were loaded with sacks. Sometimes Grandfather would come out of his shed and quiet those who wept. Grandmother was a short woman, withdrawn, and her movements were restrained and quick. Her contact with the people was quiet, without unnecessary gestures. Sometimes she would serve tea to those who were waiting. Those who wished to see the rabbi would present sacks of flour, vegetables, and bottles of oil. If their donation was too much, Grandfather would step out of his shed the next day and scold them. A rabbi is not a lord. He doesn't eat more than he needs. You should give to the poor and the sick. There are many such people in the villages. At times like this Grandfather would seem like an ancient prophet.

The local commissars of the Communist movement shrewdly cast their spell over the young and drew them from their houses. Later, they would take them away to training camps. The best of them, and there were many, were sent to the Soviet Union. Prayers and pleas were of no use, nor was the intervention of the aged rabbi. They were seduced and left their homes and never returned. How did we sin? At night in the courtyard they would ring their hands and implore. Grandfather would stand in the doorway, mute as a stone.

During those long bright summers, I learned the morning, afternoon, and evening prayers. Grandmother would sit and practice with me. She knew the prayers by heart. Sometimes we practiced so long that I would fall asleep on the porch. Grandfather seldom spoke to me. It was clear that he didn't know how to talk to children.

Mother didn't ask at the end of the summer how it was or what Grandfather had said. I myself did not yet know how being in the forest had changed me. At night I would remember the tall, bearded men who gathered at the door of Grandfather's house. Their sturdiness belied a certain helplessness. They expected the rabbi to say something to them, but since he said nothing, they would shift in place like tethered horses. Grandfather, hearing their dismay, would leave his shed and cry out, "Prayer and charity will ward off the evil decree. Go to the poor and give them the fruits of the season." Then they would immediately mount their wagons, snap their whips on the backs of the horses, and be swallowed up by the darkness.

When my father heard about my visit to Grandfather he said, "Why did you go there?" As if I had gone to a place I was too young for. Of course, he immediately realized it wasn't my fault, and he blamed my mother.

When I was in my father's care, I didn't go to school. Father would say, "Bourgeois education spoils the natural instincts. Besides, it's better for a child to be among working people. He can learn what life is from them."

THE IRON TRACKS

I spent most of the months with my father on trains, in third class, of course, with all the wretched and oppressed, crossing through villages, rivers, and forests. He loved the Ruthenian way of life from the depths of his soul, and he would pronounce every word in their language as if savoring a piece of honey cake. The Ruthenians were impressed by his accent, but they guessed, of course, that he wasn't one of their own. In the party cells, father was well known. He was chairman of every meeting. I was silent witness to all the plans and plots that were hatched in closed sessions. Here they planned their acts of sabotage and arson. In particular, they harassed Jewish factory owners, who paid their workers little and late.

Life in stables, near the animals, was for me a lasting magic. I very much wanted to stay awake to hear all the new words that flew at those meetings, but as soon as the pungent odors struck my nostrils, I would collapse into sleep.

When I was seven my father went underground. For years afterward he went without daylight. We lived in tunnels, caves, abandoned houses, and barns on the outskirts of villages. During these times he didn't talk with me much. In fact, he was so absorbed in his work that he seemed unaware of my existence. From his hiding places he organized strikes, acts of arson, demonstrations, and more. Then I realized the extent of his hostility toward the Jewish factory owners. He saw Jewish shops as the very source of evil. Without hesitation, he would send them up in flames. There were a number of Jews among the underground members, but they were just like Ruthenians, speaking their language and making their gestures. Like father, they hated the merchants. In those years I learned the scent of the earth and the fragrance of barley and corn. In every corner there was a mat to curl up on. Sometimes my father would awaken in the middle of the night and ask, "Where are you? Are you cold?" I knew that he had had a nightmare.

When the police were after him, he would leave me with a peasant, the way you would a tame animal that there's no need to tether. The peasant would go out to the fields in the morning, and I would remain in the courtyard. In the evening, when I would ask, "Where's Father?" the peasant would raise his head, stare at me with some anger, and say, "How would I know?" When Father would appear in the middle of the night, there was no end to my joy.

Sometimes he would wake me up and say, "You should go to school. Everybody goes to school." These were old words that slipped out of his mouth by mistake. His true opinion was clear: a bourgeois school corrupts thought, and it's best to remain far from its walls.

For months I was dragged along with him. There was not a village in the region that we missed. In time I learned that the district where we were hiding was, in fact, a small swampy area that was almost uninhabited. The constant movement from place to place made me forget my mother's face and our humble house in the city. When I finally returned to her she looked at me with sadness and asked, "Where have you been, my dear?"

"In the villages."

"You didn't go to school?"

"No."

My mother bowed her head. I felt that the changes in me hurt her, but she didn't say a word, as if she understood that what had been done could not be undone.

I refused to go to school. In my wanderings with my father I had gotten used to dark places, and sudden light startled me. I looked forward to my father's arrival, but for some reason he was slow to come. More and more, my life was confined to sitting in the yard or next to the window. In vain my mother tried to speak to me. The words that left her mouth sounded alien and artificial. Once I said to her, "Why don't you speak Ukrainian?" Hearing that criticism, she bowed her head, as if her hidden wound had been opened again.

CHAPTER

9

After three hours of rapid travel the train stops at Pracht.
This is a small village on a hill surrounded by pines. I discovered the village at the start of my wanderings, and
since then I do not pass it by. I suffered then from severe
ulcers and was compelled to stop over even in remote
stations. In Pracht I found a simple inn, but one fur-
nished, if I may say so, with great thought: a large bed,
a bathtub, and a window facing the meadows. Only in

Pracht does my body cease its gallop. There I close my eyes and plunge into sleep. The presence of the owner, Mrs. Groton, a tall, aristocratic woman, is barely felt. Her soft steps are lightly absorbed by the peasant carpets. Were it not for the fears that drive me from place to place, I would remain here. In Pracht, I forget my legs, my weariness subsides, and I sink into dreamless sleep. Dreams have always been my enemy. There are dreams that grip me with such force that I have no choice but to get up in the middle of the night and flee for my life. A bench in a public park is better than these garish nightmares. In Pracht the dreams peel away from me, like a scab from a healed wound. After two days of uninterrupted slumber, my head is cleared of all visions, and I stand in the courtyard, empty, as if after a long illness.

Mrs. Groton usually prepares breakfast for me on the porch. If it is raining, I sit in the dining alcove. We speak little, but she understands me even without words. All her movements are calm and silent. When I stand in the courtyard and see her next to the well, washing or hanging out the laundry, I understand that life is more than evil haste. Mrs. Groton—I feel the need to call out to her by name—what is the secret you conceal within yourself? I, of course, stifle my voice. I stand there and follow her measured movements, as if trying to decipher a code.

In Pracht I sit and plan my moves. From here I try to pick up the trail of Nachtigel, the murderer of my parents. I have no doubt that he's to be found in this region. Several times already I have gotten close to him, but he, with great cunning, managed to slip away. Most likely he lives in comfort, in a small, whitewashed house, surrounded by lawns and rose beds. I know that he was, when all is said and done, a minor murderer. Arch-murderers also live here undisturbed. But I have sworn that I will not rest until I find him. The thought that he is within striking distance excites me, and I prepare and hope I will stand the test.

Years ago Mrs. Groton mentioned, by chance, that a man named Nachtigel stayed with her for a week. He was sixty, a quiet man, who sat with his papers most of the day and seemed to be an agent for a well-known firm. The last night he got drunk and revealed to her that during the war he was in the East and was involved in hunting down Jews. On the basis of her impressions, and from what I know, I have no doubt that he was the murderer Nachtigel. If I were capable of sealing off the area I would trap him, but in this tranquil, green expanse, it's hard enough to find a house even with a precise address.

I have not given up. On the contrary, in recent years the desire to find him has grown even stronger. Were it not for my tendency to oversleep, my unwarranted fears, and my confusing nightmares, I would already have found him. Nevertheless, all is not in vain. I have several comrades who are on his trail, and they too are certain that the day is not far when we shall find him. Since I revealed to Mrs. Groton that I'm a Jew, she looks upon me with a kindly eye, serves me crisp toast for breakfast, good coffee, and cheesecake for dessert.

She was born in Prague. In her youth she worked in the university administration, where she knew many Jewish students. Now, when she recalls them, a girlish smile lights her face. Like me, she hates the Austrians and fears them. Were she younger, she would return to her native city. I, for my part, promise her that after we liquidate the murderer, I'll bring her to Prague. Thus we weave our plans.

In the meantime, the years pass. Old age has crept up on Mrs. Groton, and also on me, and Nachtigel, who was at times within reach, no longer roams alone in these parts. In the evenings Mrs. Groton sits and tells me about the days of her youth. At that time the Jews were the un-crowned nobility of Prague. Her first suitor was Jewish, a tall, handsome fellow who would write poems and read them to her. When her parents heard of it, they forbade her to see him, but the poor fellow took a chance and came to ask their permission. They slammed the door in his face. At that time she was young and didn't dare stand up to her parents. In the end, she married an Austrian and moved to Austria.

The quiet in her house soothes my nerves. Some-times I imagine I'll spend my last years here, among the tall trees that cast their long shadows on the earth. Here I will join all those beloved by me. I will not forget the women who showed kindness to me. Something of them lives within me. Even for a woman whom I paid to lie with me for a night, I retain a certain spark. At night, when the trains are empty and the black wind howls through the cracks, I curl up in my coat and think about them and join them once again.

A year ago Mrs. Groton surprised me and said, "No one knows when his final hour will come. I want to give you something very dear to me."

"Why?" I was apprehensive.

"Because you're the only one who will preserve it." She removed the objects from her coat pocket and placed it on the table. It was a thin mezuza, decorated with Hebrew letters.

"That's a sacred object." I trembled.

"I'll tell you something I've never revealed to anyone," she said, bowing her head. "My maternal grandmother was Jewish, and she converted. Before she died she gave this to my mother, who in turn left it to me. Now the time has come to pass it on. I'm giving it to you for you're a Jew."

"Not a believing Jew," I hastened to explain.

"Still, it's better for it to be with you. This amulet once calmed me."

"How?"

"I don't know. But in the past year it's begun to burden me. A sign that my life is nearing the end, don't you think?"

"How can I keep this? I have no house, and I wander from place to place."

"Then to whom shall I leave it?" she asked with both annoyance and authority.

I knew I couldn't refuse her. In that moment she was a person doing what she had to do, without regret. I nearly said: Only in your house do I sleep without dreams. Where will I rest now? I tried to pay her, but she refused. "If you keep this amulet, that will be my reward." She seemed to be entrusting me with some mysterious task. I wanted to excuse myself. But when I saw her open face, I didn't dare say no.

I had planned to stay at her inn another day, but my emotions prevented me. Before I left the house she kissed me on the forehead and wished me a long life. Her face was bright, her gaze pure, and her movements were flawless. Still, my throat closed, and I fled as if for my life.

Now a year has gone by, and once again I am in the station in Pracht. I stand, but my legs won't support me. I'm afraid to ask what has happened to her. Fear paralyzes me, and I sit in the neglected station swallowing drink after drink, waiting for the next train.

10

From here on only the express runs, and the distance from station to station is long. I sink into the soft seats and know that this is my home. I have no other. There are, I must admit, also a few pleasant surprises in this motion: a familiar shadow, a sudden scent, sometimes a tune that draws me back, irresistibly, to childhood. When I'm fortunate, I meet one of my rivals on this line. For a while he tries to lose me, but I won't give in. In the end I trap him in a dark corner.

It turns out that I'm mistaken. He's not a rival of mine. On the contrary, like me, he is also tracking down Nachtigel. He's been after him for years. True, in the past year he's grown weary, begun to sleep a lot, and when things got tough he turned to the Australian consulate and asked for a visa. Now he's sorry. You mustn't break a vow, particularly an oath. I tell him of my discoveries and about my comrades, who secretly track him. It turns out that some of them are his partners too. For instance, he knows Mrs. Groton. Like me, he admires her and her humble inn. We have a drink, warm up, and reminisce. His route does not usually overlap with mine, but sometimes he happens into this region. For a few years he lived in Weinberg, but he can't bear the anti-Semitic remarks anymore. He prefers to live far from the stations. We spoke of Stark, of course. Upon hearing Stark's name he grimaced and said, "It's hard for me to stomach Jewish Communists. Their devotion reminds me of the other kind of piety. Let them reform themselves first and then the world." But why waste words? They no longer exist. They are just shadows, ghosts. We have a task in life: we must find the murderer. After we find him, we can quietly emigrate to Australia.

Incidentally, a few years ago I met Rollman's nephew on this express. What a resemblance he bears to his uncle. He was on his way to France. Twenty-seven, and all the characteristics of a Jewish Communist were stamped on his face: the flash in the eyes, the determination, the furtiveness. I wanted to stop him for a moment, but he wouldn't listen. I couldn't restrain myself and called out, "I knew your uncle Rollman well. I was with him in his final hours. Where are you headed?"

"To Paris."

"You're leaving this region?"

"This place is a wasteland. In France there is true labor."

"Why don't we have a drink in the buffet?"

"I'm in a rush. The committee is meeting in Paris tonight. Excuse me."

That brief contact with Rollman's nephew restored his face and his death to me in a single stroke. Jewish Communists are born with a death wish. First in the underground, then in prison. In the Soviet Union they weren't executed before they confessed. Still, my father defended passionately everything that was done there. If a comrade challenged the leadership, he would be called before the committee, and there he would confess, admit his mistakes. My mother didn't speak much. But her mute face said, Nothing will force us to abandon our commitment to reforming the world.

Since I left Stark, his face has not abandoned me. His eyes beckon me from the distance: "Come back, we

are a small family, scattered, and we must look out for
one another. I did what I could. Now I can do no more.
But my faith in a better world has not been marred, even
now. We sacrificed the life of the present for the future,
and I left this world without resentment. In a few generations people will remember us and say, Jewish Communism was the true Communism. Everyone was devoted,
heart and soul, to the end." Thus I hear his voice. And
at night, when the darkness gathers, I see his chiseled
features and shrink into my corner because I abandoned him.

In Sternberg the express stops. Some stations
make me race straight to the buffet. In others I descend
as if they weren't stations at all, but places enveloped in
light, where one must tread cautiously. Sternberg is a
medium-sized station, surrounded by warehouses, and
in the back is a pleasant, tidy buffet. In that buffet, more
than twenty years ago, I discovered my beloved, Bertha.
She was a tall, attractive woman who worked at the cash
register. At first she tried to avoid my gaze, but that eva-
sion merely confirmed my suspicion: she was one of
ours. I told her a few of my secrets. She told me about
herself. I learned to love her body and to honor her si-
lences. There was an episode in her life that she would
not talk about, but she spoke about the rest freely, even
gaily. Her movements were fluid, not those of someone
who had been in the camps. At first her movements

scared me, but over the years I learned to respect them. I
know the limits of devotion, and I won't ask for more.
People like us are bound to many others, living and dead.
Do not ask for unnecessary devotion from your fellow
man. With this in mind, I proposed marriage to her years
ago. I was thirty-five, weary of the trains, and my body
yearned for a permanent bed. Bertha looked at me with
wide eyes as if to say: Why should we perpetrate that in-
justice on one another? You must be on the road, and I
need solitude. The candor of her gaze astounded me. After that we saw each other just once a year, at the end of
May, actually from the twenty-third to the end of the
month. Like all of us, she aged a little over the years, but
her fine features did not fade. Her broad smile seemed to
say, I won't allow sadness to overcome me.

If she had accompanied me on my journeys, it
would have been easier for me. The night train is gloomy,
when all is said and done. We could have enjoyed ourselves together in the stations. True, I have obligations
that I must not involve Bertha in, a few matters best left to
silence. Yes, it would have been different. I tried to persuade her, but unsuccessfully. A year ago she surprised
me and said, "I have decided to return to my hometown,
to Zalishtshik."

"What possesses you?" I trembled.

"I must go," she said without joy.

THE IRON TRACKS

"There are no Jews there, only Ukrainians and Poles."

She had hinted to me before that she was thinking about returning to her hometown. She spoke of longings and obligations, but I saw it as a whim. Once I even scolded her and said, "One doesn't return to a city that is a cemetery. There's a limit to the mourning that a person can endure."

All night long I tried to persuade her that the journey was untimely and dangerous, that she should postpone it. I even promised that I would sell some jewels and travel with her. For a moment it seemed that those words had touched her heart. She gave me a cup of coffee and some cookies, and chatted with me about many things, among them a wanderer who had happened into the buffet. He turned out to be a Jew from Galicia. In the morning he wrapped himself in a prayer shawl and prayed. I knew she was just trying to distract me. The dreadful course was already set in her head.

Still, I tried again to dissuade her from traveling. I spoke about the obligations we have here, about the people who need us, like Stark and Mina, and about the duty to find the murderers and kill them. As long as they live, our lives are not lives. As always, superficial words and words of truth got jumbled together. Now I realize I should have joined her, but then, for some reason, I was sure that my life here had another purpose. I secretly hoped she would change her mind the next morning. But I had not yet grasped the depth of her abyss.

Next day, in the station, as we each waited for our own train, the words fell unsaid within me. Bertha spoke to me as if I were a younger brother, beaten, who has lost his way. Her eyes shone fiercely, like those of a person who no longer fears death.

In the spring I learned that my Bertha had reached Zalishtshik and rented a room from a peasant woman. She spends most of the day on a riverbank, and for now she does not plan to return. This information came from a Jewish merchant who had traveled to Zalishtshik to pray at his ancestors' tombs. To my question whether she was content, he answered coarsely in a voice that frightened me, "Very content."

Now Sternberg is no longer Sternberg for me, just a burning space where one must not linger. Still, I step up to the buffet and ask the owner, "Have you heard from Bertha?"

"Not a word."

I sit on the bench where we used to sit together before and after every trip. Since she left me, my hold on the world has become weaker.

CHAPTER

11

The trip north from Sternberg is like a plunge into cold
water. Bertha's face remains before me. The thought that
she is sitting on the riverbank for most of the day, gazing
at the water, speaking to no one, that thought—rather,
that image—gradually takes on a blue hue. It is a frigid
blue, which recalls to my heart columns of silent men
bearing heavy packs on their backs. I should have aban-

doned this circuit and gone to draw her out of her trance. It would have been better for her to throw in her lot with me than to founder as she has done. I say "I should have," but with me everything is delayed, hesitant. For years I have been bound to this circuit, and now that Bertha can no longer be reached by train, I'm drawn to her all the more.

A year ago, right after I parted from Bertha, on this very line I met a tall woman who could have been her double. She sat across from me reading a book. I instantly felt an attraction. I wasn't mistaken. One of us. When I turned to her, she made a strange gesture of refusal. It seems she was deaf. I'm not put off by deaf people. I have a close friend, completely deaf, who lives not far from here.

I wrote her a note in my mother tongue: my name and the name of my hometown. She answered in a clear hand, "We are neighbors. My name is Rosa Tag, and I am from Strozhnitz." Had it not been for her handicap, we would have settled into conversation. On a train conversation can be as good as cognac. Once I spent time with Father in a pigsty not far from Strozhnitz. I did not enter the town itself.

I continued to write, "Where were you during the war?"

"In Siberia," she answered. I understood: from a wealthy family. When the Russians invaded us in the forties, they exiled the rich to Siberia. Most of them became sick and died there, and the rest froze and returned as invalids. I am fond of deaf women, but it is hard for me to embrace them. For some reason they seem childlike to me, defenseless.

I wrote out Bertha's name for her, and she answered, "I don't remember her." I sat and contemplated her face. Contemplation, I have learned, is a kind of absorption. When I contemplate, my entire being is aroused, as when I hear good music.

Nevertheless, I couldn't restrain myself. I told her that she was very similar to my friend Bertha, who had just returned to her native city of Zalishtshik. Her answer moved me: "My mother was born in Zalishtshik."

"Now we're bound to each other, and not by chance," I wrote.

"If I had money, I would go back, too," she answered.

"You must not become addicted to fantasies," I scolded her. "A fantasy is more dangerous than cognac. A person must do the right thing, without submitting a bill or expecting a reward."

I trembled at the words that I wrote and wanted to take them back. I hate rhetoric. I remembered that those were my father's words, he used to recite them to me. Years ago I had grievances against him. Now my relationship with him is calm, and on the platforms I find more and more people like him.

The train stopped in Gruendorf. I kissed her hand in the old-fashioned way. Now I'm sorry I didn't ask her where she lived. I should have invited her for a meal in the buffet. One does not leave a woman behind without making such a gesture.

I regard Gruendorf as a crossroads. Every time I arrive there, I am filled again with the will to live. Perhaps that is because of my secret comrade, Mrs. Braun, a tall, sturdy woman whose movements are those of a fugitive. Her nervousness attracted my eye at once, and I foolishly asked her, "Where did you pick up those gestures?"

"From my father," she said.

"And who was your father?"

"A Jew," she whispered. "But my mother was not."

Since then we've been friends. Her husband, a native of the region, works in the forest, and she manages the buffet. I saw him just once. His face was closed and tense, like that of a man about to bring his whip down on a stubborn animal. Once she revealed to me: He drinks too much.

When she's in good spirits, she tells me about the war, how she lived in a shack near the sawmill, how she insisted on going to church, and how she prayed every night to an icon. She was afraid of informers, and even now she is frightened. Hatred for the Jews is strong in this region, and even though there is hardly a Jew to be found, everybody talks about them as if they were alive and well.

Years ago, in a moment of grace, I revealed to her that I was tracking down Nachtigel and asked for her help. She knows the region well, who took part in the war and who stayed behind. On Saturday nights and Sundays people from all over gather in her buffet. They argue and get drunk and stir up wartime memories. In time Mrs. Braun also confirmed my hunch, that indeed a man named Nachtigel is sometimes to be found here, and indeed he was one of the murderers. For every scrap of information I pay her or give her a present. Once she confessed to me, "Your gifts are very dear to me. They arouse a Jewish sentiment in me." I don't believe her. Lately, I've even stopped believing the information she supplies. She, like her husband, has taken to drink in recent years, and since then she has been imagining things. She turns hunches into statements of fact, takes liberties with past and present, and tells me "true" stories that never happened. But it's hard for me to be angry with her. In moments of abandon, she risks telling me that her loyalty to the Jews is absolute. Although she's only half

Jewish, she feels completely Jewish. She promises me that one day she will leave that accursed region, board an express, and ride straight to Israel.

I know these are fantasies. As soon as she sobers up, she forgets all about them. Still, I enjoy hearing them. Once she turned to me and said, "What are you doing here? I don't understand you. Here everything is corrupt. Take the first train and go to Israel."

"And who will kill Nachtigel?"

"I," she said. "I will do it in your place."

Whenever anyone mentions Israel, I am filled with gloom. I would very much like to go there, to gather strength. I would then return here fortified. A month in Israel would make me a brave man. It would teach me to get away from the trains and live in the forest. There I would learn to concentrate, to stay on the track, and not to despair. Silence. That is what I need. And that is just what you can't have on trains. Trains, in the end, are just a tangle of nerves.

This time she noticed me right at the entrance to the buffet and called out, "Here he is, the solace of my soul." Right away she served me borscht with sour cream and a cheese omelette. She knew I like those foods. I, for my part, brought her a silk handkerchief. She was very pleased with it and started telling me about people and rumors. Among other things, a fact: Nachtigel bought a house in Weinberg that is being renovated.

"You doubted me," she said provocatively. "But I haven't forgotten my mission. My ears are always open, and I ask questions."

"Thank you," I said.

"You mustn't thank me. I owe something to the Jewish people, don't I?"

That's how Mrs. Braun is. In recent years it has been hard to rely on her, but when she's sober, a kind of honesty returns to her eyes. This is a look that stores pain. Once she said to me, "My father was unhappy with me because I never finished high school. That hurt him a lot. Even on his deathbed it grieved him. I did make an effort, but I didn't have the composure to concentrate. I was involved with boys and didn't do my homework. In the end there was no choice but to send me to a vocational school. That was a day of mourning for my father. My mother, on the other hand, wasn't very sorry. 'If she doesn't want to study, why force her? Work is nothing to be ashamed of.' Father didn't agree, but he didn't quarrel. Now I feel his sorrow. He was a quiet man and neither my mother nor I was afraid of him."

Mrs. Braun wins me over, and I forgive her for the nonsense she serves up, for the loans that she will never pay back. Clearly, she is no angel from heaven. Still, there is a kind of light in her soul.

The next day I go to the fair. The fair here reminds me of my hometown and the bright summertime lights that stayed lit until midnight. Here, too, the nights are lit up, but I feel nothing.

Two hundred years ago Jews lived in this poor town. Their memory has been erased, but in the market I once found a few Jewish antiques that moved me very much. Since then I make sure to come here on a market day. Occasionally I remain in the area for a week or two, so I can return for the Tuesday fair. I've never revealed this to Mrs. Braun. I suspect that if she knew the value of the objects, she would be tempted to buy them out from under me. She's no fool.

In this remote fair, over the years, I've found wine goblets, candlesticks, menorahs, and even an old prayer book. When I showed the book to Stark, he was very moved. His eyes filled with tears. Stark is a creature of a very special sort, the kind of person that is now extinct in the world.

This is my strange way of making a living. I buy antiques whose value no one here can estimate, and I sell them to collectors. I guard this secret zealously. I have eager competitors who sometimes get there first, but mostly I beat them to it. In my valise I keep a schedule of all the fairs in the region, and my life follows its dictates. Because of the fairs I am forced to drag myself to distant places, but it pays off. No pleasure is like that of discovering an antique.

THE IRON TRACKS

Once Stark told me, "Your work is holy. You mustn't leave these precious objects in the hands of strangers. Marvelous memories are stored up in them." Since he said that to me, my attraction to these godforsaken places has grown stronger. Sometimes my heart chides me for that devotion because it can distract me from my main goal: the murderer.

CHAPTER

12

I know the town of Gruendorf and the surrounding villages like the palm of my hand. Here I sometimes stay
until autumn. Occasionally I go as far as the mountains.
True, I don't always find what I'm looking for. The fairs
are mostly wretched and depressing, but the landscape in
this season makes up for them. Between one village and
another is everything to nourish the soul: blue skies,

green meadows, and oak-lined paths. The silence here envelops. I forget the ulcer that gnaws at me. But not Bertha's face. Now that she is mortifying herself, far away on a riverbank, I find myself drawn to her with an irresistible force.

Between one village and the next I take out my bottle of cognac. Thus I drive away the dismal clouds and the burning dread. Without cognac, the sights of Wirblbahn return to me. Once again I see the horrors of my rebirth, and life no longer has any meaning. But if fortune smiles upon me, I discover treasures wherever I turn. Seven years ago I returned to the station from here with two bulging rucksacks. What didn't I find! Candlesticks, two Hanukkah menorahs, and many wine goblets. Most valuable of all: the books. An old peasant displayed a pile of antique books in an old basin. I immediately saw that they were treasures worth their weight in gold. So as not to arouse his suspicion, I also bought other things.

Indeed I found a treasure trove, a prayer book from the seventeenth century among it. Its edges were frayed, but the letters were clear, the parchment binding well preserved, and on it, in clear handwriting, were written folk cures, memorial days of relatives, and even a few sketches, showing that children studied from this book. My Hebrew and Aramaic are limited, but my strange dealings over the years have forced me to learn them. At first I would buy and sell without knowing what I was doing. Then Rabbi Zimmel, of whom I will have more to say, sat me down in the schoolroom. That was many years ago, when I had just begun my searches, or rather when I was still blundering through mazes. Once, by chance, in an antique shop in an Italian village, I bought an illuminated Haggadah. Although the drawings had faded, the letters had retained their color. When I showed it to Rabbi Zimmel, he took his head in his hands and cried out, "From the thirteenth century!"

Rabbi Zimmel then paid me a decent sum for the Haggadah, and I promised him I would learn Hebrew. But I haven't made much progress, it's hard for me to lug the heavy dictionary by Grozowski in my valise, and at night I'm tired. Though a few books are to be found in my valise, and I occasionally look at them, I truly study only with Rabbi Zimmel.

The treasure trove contained valuable and rare books, Kabbalistic and homiletic works. When I piled them on his desk, Rabbi Zimmel hugged me and said, "These are treasures. I'll write to Gershom Scholem in Jerusalem, and he will come to visit me."

Fortune does not favor me every year. There are years when I drag my feet from fair to fair and find only desolation. Tattered schoolbooks are displayed on the stands, and the storerooms are piled with rotten furniture. Old horses brought for sale droop near the fences, and their owners, in their boredom, whip them mercilessly.

Having no other escape, I flee to the water and sit at the edge of the lake, observing the noisy flight of wild geese. That doesn't always help. When melancholy attacks me in the field, I must drug it immediately. Sometimes I have no alternative but to down a whole bottle. I get drunk and crumple like a sack.

After seven or eight hours of steady sleep I wake up, open my eyes, and a kind of clarity extends before me like a horizon. The whole area, its hills and valleys, is presented to me as if on an outstretched hand. Then I hear a voice saying to me, "Why don't you go to Jugendorf? There's no fair there, but books and objects are sold in the square in front of the local council. Get up and go there." That voice has never fooled me. Two years ago I found a pair of candlesticks in Jugendorf. Though they weren't antiques, their beauty touched my heart.

Thus have I wandered for many years now. My rivals are also to be found in the region, and sometimes I run into one of them. They're less knowledgeable than I. They go about in confusion, and in the end I see them looking discouraged, lying under an oak tree.

It's clear that the treasures grow scarcer from year to year, and it's likely that in a few years there won't be any left. But I'm not worried. What I find not only supports me, but fills me with excitement. My zeal to get to the right place, to discover and buy, completely overwhelms me. On this front I'm a perfect soldier. Over the years I've learned to heed myself, to listen to my senses, to rise and eagerly follow my feet, straight to the hiding place. This is a skill that I've developed on my own, and the results surprise me every time all over again. Thus in musty cellars I have found Passover dishes decorated with Hebrew letters, wine goblets, and candlesticks. In remote fairs that seem at first glance to be lacking anything cultural, I have found old books and manuscripts. Rabbi Zimmel once told me that the day would come when people will speak of my discoveries the way they speak of the Cairo Geniza. Certainly his enthusiasm was exaggerated, but the appetite for pursuing and finding these treasures draws me out of my gloom. When I do uncover something, there is no limit to my joy.

Years ago Rabbi Zimmel told me that if this region is emptied of its treasures, I would do well to turn to another territory, Germany perhaps. I hope that my experience, which I acquired by dint of hard work, will stand me in good stead there as well. Age, I see, doesn't diminish that hidden sense. On the contrary, now I discover hiding places more easily. I have never discussed this ability with anyone, not even Bertha. Only Rabbi Zimmel, only he knows the secret.

But in the end the darkness is greater than the light. Perhaps it would be better to say, longer. When darkness descends upon me, I am lost and sick in this green desert. There is a reason for this: the smell of the vegetation in this season, especially the poppies, stifles me. There seems to be no air like Gruendorf's, and during my first stays here I didn't even realize why. But now I know: it is the subtle fragrance that rises from the poppies. An odorless smell, a smell that has no obvious sign, but that directly works on the nervous system. In the past I used to try to flee from the place immediately, but I soon learned that flight was of no use. On the contrary, running away just increased the effect. So I choose a mountain ridge, a place the winds rush through, and only there does the smell abate. I have learned that everything is tied together. A season without poppies is a successful season. My senses aren't disturbed; my senses and my feet are coordinated. I reach the places I have to reach.

Sometimes, when the patches of darkness join together, I take the pistol out of my valise and fire a magazine full of bullets into the air. I found the pistol in Wirblbahn right after the war. If fate brings Nachtigel to me, I'll shoot him calmly, without doubt or anger. I prepare myself for that moment even in my sleep.

After shooting I sit quietly, clean the gun, and contemplate it for a long time. I feel that it will serve me at the right moment. By the way, I've told only one person of its existence. Once, in an odd moment, Bertha anxiously asked, "Why don't you have a pistol? You wander the roads, and you ought to be able to defend yourself." I was about to reveal the secret to her, but I held back.

Years ago a tenant attacked Mrs. Groton. He spoke to her roughly and threatened to kill Mutzi, her little dog, because he had awakened him at night. Mrs. Groton turned pale and begged his pardon. Full of fear, she explained to him that Mutzi was a quiet, polite dog, and had only cried because of a wound on his foot. That explanation did not satisfy the tenant. He continued to speak rudely and threatened her again. As soon as I saw that he really intended to kill Mrs. Groton's poor little creature, I headed for my room so that I could come back and threaten him with the pistol. Fortunately, he had changed his mind, paid, and left.

The pistol is one of my precious secrets. I don't have many opportunities to take care of it. Just here, in these uninhabited spaces, I unwrap it in the evening, take it apart, clean it with a soft rag, oil the delicate barrel, and put it back in its place.

When the season displeases me, I head north to the barren Graten Mountains. I go most of the way on foot, but
if it rains hard, I hire a wagon and ride up. When I first
told Rabbi Zimmel about my trips there, he remarked,
"In that place, as far as I know, Jews never lived." But I,
for some reason, am drawn there. I readily obey my legs;
never have they deceived me. Once they revealed Stark's

hiding place to me. By means of them I discovered the good fairs, and even my Bertha. My thoughts are always full of conflict, my feelings about to explode. Only my legs have composure.

The Graten Mountains are high but not steep, and they extend over a large area. At the end of summer a dense silence hangs there, completely intoxicating me. I rent a room from a peasant woman, Gretchen, and I sleep. When I first came to her she still worked in the fields. Her married daughters would come from far away and visit her. They would sit together outdoors and chat late into the night. Occasionally I, too, would join them. Now she's eighty, her face has shriveled, but when she wears her straw hat in the garden, her youth returns to her face, and she hoes the flower beds with spryness.

In the evening she serves me cottage cheese in sour cream, a salad of garden vegetables, and fresh village bread. She is a simple woman, and her ideas are limited, but when she talks about her garden, about the cow that no longer gives milk in abundance, about the dog that died an untimely death, and about her daughters who no longer visit her as in the past, her words have a kind of hidden wisdom. I know that, unlike me, she has always been close to plants and animals, and from them she has drawn vitality. Now, in her old age, she speaks about her death in a natural way, as if she knows when her day will come. I ask her various questions because I like to hear her voice. There is nothing superfluous in her words. What she knows from her experience, she tells me, without affectation or pretense.

A year ago, when I told her I was Jewish, she was surprised, but she didn't burden me with questions. That evening I realized that the information had stunned her. Though she continued to serve me meals with the same care, she no longer sat beside me. A kind of sadness that I had not seen before began to register in her face. Gretchen, I wanted to tell her, if my presence disturbs you, I'll look for another place. Your old age is precious to me, and I wouldn't want to bring any distress to it.

She apparently understood my expression, and at a certain point seemed about to apologize, but her aversion was obviously too strong for her to overcome. Jews, I had learned, are intimidating, and now that they are absent their memory arouses a kind of hidden panic. Once a whore on a night train confided to me that she was willing to sleep with any man, in any place, but not with a Jew. Jews cast a pall over her appetites, and it was hard for her to abide her body afterward.

"How do you know who is a Jew?" I feigned innocence.

"They're circumcised, didn't you know?" She betrayed her foolishness.

Last year, when I left Gretchen, I didn't say, "Until we see each other again," and she didn't see me out as usual. I knew that she didn't want to see me again.

But life is not only failures, it turns out. As I was leaving her house, I saw, as in a bad dream, a short, bearded man coming up from the valley. I couldn't believe my eyes and drew closer to him. Indeed, he was a Jew.

"What's a Jew doing here?" I blurted.

"I live here," he answered quietly.

It turned out that not far away, in an isolated house, he and his wife lived with their seven children. Later he told me their story. They had been brought here during the war, and here they had been saved. He hasn't left since. They keep a little shop and an inn for travelers. His faith was embodied in all his manners, even in the way he looked at his children. His wife was short and thin, and it was hard to believe that her belly had borne seven children.

"Do you come from an observant home?" I asked.

"No."

Religious Jews frighten me. They are very conspicuous, and it is easy to identify them. More than once over the years, in remote railway stations, I wanted to approach one of them and whisper in his ear, Your appearance gives you away. Why wear a yarmulke? Why? But

I didn't feel this man was in danger. His movements were calm, and his face serene. The children surrounded him with softness and sheltered him. I told him that I came there once a year, that I stayed with Gretchen and hiked in the countryside. I was glad he didn't ask about my business. When people do that, my insides shrivel up. His house reminded me of Grandfather's house, which was also suffused with calm. Only a believer, it seems, knows tranquility.

"How did you attain faith?" I ventured into his territory and immediately regretted it. He looked at his wife, and the two of them looked at me as if to say, We cannot answer that. If we say that we felt it was the only way we could live after the camps, would we have conveyed anything? And if we added that we felt this place was entrusted to us, and that we had to preserve it, would that be understood?

Later he told me that he intended, in another year, to sell what he could and emigrate to Jerusalem. The period of isolation was ending, and the time had come to rejoin the Jewish people. The words were familiar to me, and I understood their meaning. Despite that a barrier descended between us, divided us in silence.

Meanwhile, he told me that in the past year some hooligans had poured kerosene on his house with intentions of setting it afire. Had it not been for the brave dogs that attacked them, the house would have burned down. "You need a pistol," I said.

We talked until late at night. It turned out that they had been in the same labor camp I was in, they had worked in the same "pits," but they remembered more than I did. They not only remembered Stark and Mina, but also my Bertha. When I told them that Bertha had gone back to her hometown, they weren't surprised. They told me that she had spoken about her parents with great longing. The hospitality of these people showed me how cut off I was from this world, as if I had lost everything, even my few memories.

That night I didn't sleep. I was angry that Gretchen, whose ways I admired and still admire, had estranged herself from me, as if she had discovered in me an unforgivable flaw. Though she had made no insulting remark, all of her being had said, Something about you isn't right. Maybe it's not your fault, but still it's hard to bear the presence of someone so hideously flawed within. It seemed that because of me her blue eyes had changed color and become metallic so as to have the power to drive me out of her life, which was nearing its end.

CHAPTER

14

On the train north from Gruendorf I learned of Stark's death. One of my rivals approached and informed me. "No!" I cried out without thinking. He was a short Jew with a tired expression who turns up in certain villages after me. I have even seen him in the Graten Mountains. His presence always annoys me. More than once I have nearly warned him not to follow in my tracks, not to undermine me. Now he stood before me like a scolded brother.

"When did you hear?" I asked, and I immediately felt that my world had been destroyed.

"Regularly, year after year, I would visit him at the end of July," he answered in slightly formal language, as if he were an attendant in a funeral parlor. From close up he looked frightening: the camp smell still clings to his clothes.

"He was like a father to me," I said and rose to my feet. "I was with him just two and a half months ago."

"He was forsaken." The Jew made a strange gesture.

"We all loved him," I said.

"Only a few came to him in recent years." He didn't stop reproaching.

"And who took part in the funeral?"

"Not one of us. The nuns discovered him and buried him in the convent cemetery."

"Where are the books? Where are the manuscripts?"

"I arrived a few days after the burial. The house was open, and there was nothing inside. The Mother Superior told me that the local council had given them the building as a gift, and they were planning to renovate it."

"And the manuscripts?"

"They fumigated the house and apparently burned everything."

If the train had stopped, I would have gotten off.

Whenever the whip lands on my back, I get off, curl up in a buffet, and lick my wounds. The train raced now at full speed, and the man sitting before me took no pity on me. He answered all my questions to the point, though not without aggression, saying: "We are indeed weak creatures, frightened and self-involved. But there are times when a person must stand up for himself and confront the truth. Lies make us filthy. We abandoned him. The time has come to admit it."

I looked into his eyes and saw that his travels had given him a steady gaze. "I'm sorry," I said.

"I wasn't referring to you," he replied.

I always knew that one day my rivals would conspire against me, but I didn't imagine that this was how they would do it. The train stopped, and I got off. It turned out to be one of those barren stations where the few passengers scatter quickly, and only the locals remain on the platform. A sign with all the usual warnings stands in place.

The owner of the buffet didn't ask what I wanted to drink but served me, as he does the other customers, a mug of beer. Only then did the bitter news seep into me.

Stark, like my father, had risen through all the stages of the movement. He, too, lived underground for many years. What my father did in Bucovina, Stark did in Galicia. There, apparently, the work was more complex and dangerous. There were differences of opinion between them, I had heard, but Stark never mentioned them. Every time he recalled my father or mother he would say, "Souls with roots." He knew many secrets and wouldn't speak about certain things. In recent years he had spoken often about his father, a scion of the Hasidic dynasty of Rydzyna, who did not heed the advice of many and refused to become the Rebbe. Stark's father lived in a remote village and made a living from a grocery store. He grew vegetables in the garden with his own hands. He insisted on cleanliness and simplicity, and he would begin the day by bathing in the river. After prayers he would go out to work in the garden. He greatly regretted that his only son had joined the Communists and was intimidating the landowners and factory owners, picking especially on the Jews.

In the past few years, whenever I showed Stark a manuscript or an old book, he would sit and read, and in the end he would say, "This book would have made my father very happy." Recently it was as if the words he had used for so long had been wiped from his tongue. He now spoke in the way of his ancestors. During my last visit he reminded me of all the books I had shown him. Once I sat with him all night long, and we read *The Path of the Righteous.* When Kron, a veteran member of the party and a good friend of my father's, told him that he was speaking the way people once spoke in Jewish homes, Stark an-

swered, "My dear fellow, my forefathers, like your forefathers, were not thieves but hardworking people who
scrutinized their own conduct and gave to the poor. In
our youth we were ashamed of them and didn't see the
light in their lives, but now the time has come to admit
the truth. What did we want from them, Kron? What did
we want?"

During my last visit, Stark was very subdued, and
when I showed him a copy of *The Ethics of the Fathers* that
I had bought, he said, "That's an important book, and it
should be read with great attention and humility."

Every time the whip lands on my back, my schedule breaks down. I lose my sense of direction and forget
the people I am supposed to meet. Now I sat in the empty,
neglected station, and my world darkened around me.
The bright end of summer glimmered on the trees, and
the light was soft. But the season meant nothing to me. I
felt the sweat of my body and a weariness spreading
across my back. I hated the valise and everything it contained. My body pulled me toward sleep.

Just as I was about to close my eyes, a woman approached me and whispered in my ear, "I have a room not
far from here, a clean room with a bath. For fifty dollars
I'll spend the whole night with you. You won't be sorry,
believe me." Without desire I rose and followed her.

CHAPTER

15

The next day I thought of returning to Upper Salzstein, to
prostrate myself on Stark's tomb, and to discover the fate
of the books and manuscripts. But I was weary, confused,
and without the strength to go so far. I handed the woman
a few more banknotes and slept in her place till noon.
In the afternoon I boarded a local train and set out on
my way.

THE IRON TRACKS

A night with a woman always leaves me a bit bleary. When I was young, a night like that would merely intoxicate me, and I would immediately fall into the arms of another woman. Today one woman, even one who is not demanding, is enough for me, plunging me into a very deep sleep.

I reached the station square at two o'clock. The woman, whose name I instantly forgot, wanted to accompany me. I obliged her. She was taller than I and fat. On the platform she gave me a theatrical kiss, like someone with nothing to lose.

Toward evening I returned to Rondhof. The north is kinder to me than the south. My business here is extensive. The people are close to me and help me. They make me feel that my life is not flowing without purpose. True, years ago everything was more intense, but now, too, more than a few people work in my service.

The owner of the buffet, Mr. Drutschik, originally from Czechoslovakia, confirmed the information that Mrs. Braun had given me: that Nachtigel had bought a house in Weinberg, and it was being readied for him. I was glad. Whenever my comrades get on his trail, I feel that my life is not a waste. Mr. Drutschik is a friendly man. He likes Jews and has always longed for his homeland. I revealed my secret to him a few years ago. Since then he's been working in my service. Of course I pay him

but not very much. Once he apologized to me and said
that if his financial situation improved, he wouldn't take
a penny from me. I believe him. Meanwhile, his buffet is
meager, and the customers are few. Once his young wife
breathed life into the place, but since her sudden death
he has aged. He neglects the buffet and sits by the window
most of the day, smoking cigarettes and drinking coffee.

I am pleased that, like Mrs. Braun, he, too, has
discovered, though apparently from a different source,
that Nachtigel had bought a house in Weinberg and was
planning to live there. I ordered a drink to celebrate the
news. Drutschik told me that in the winter he happened
to be in Weinberg, and had seen the house with his
own eyes: a two-story structure surrounded by grass and
trees. To make it easier for me he drew a map: the route
from the Weinberg station to the murderer's house.
When he handed me the paper, my hands trembled. I
knew that the delay was coming to an end. The time of
testing was approaching.

Meanwhile, there were a few pressing matters: to
leave the valise in Miss Hahn's house, to shower, and to
see what they were showing at the fair. The Rondhof fair
is the largest one in the region and lasts six days. I have
found treasures there, and to tell the truth, it was there
that my life began to reveal itself. Years ago I still groped
in darkness. Now I know every hiding place, though the
main thing is to keep a sharp eye. Today I know what

every drawn sack contains, and what's in every overflowing basin. Once I surprised a peasant by asking him, "What do you have in the wagon? Why don't you show the things you have there on your stand?" His answer: "They're worthless, and not mine. They belong to my mother-in-law." Thus I found an ancient Haggadah, carefully illustrated by a Jewish artist.

Miss Hahn always greets me cordially, but this time she outdid herself, rushing toward me, hugging me, and kissing me. "You're late this time, my dear," she said. Miss Hahn is a convert to Christianity. Her parents, unlike other parents, were pleased by her decision and took part in the baptism. She was going to marry the Prince of Hohensalz. A week before the wedding, it turned out that the prince, who had spent many years in Paris, was infected with syphilis and near death. The wedding never took place, but Miss Hahn clung to Christianity. She never married and lived in seclusion like a nun. Her fondness for Jews, the rock from which she was hewn, was not concealed from me. The first time she saw me she gave me a penetrating look and said, "A Jew, if I'm not mistaken." Since then we've been friends. For breakfast she prepares toast, a soft-boiled egg, homemade cheese, and a cup of coffee. Whenever she gives me breakfast, she says, "Jews don't eat meat in the morning, I know that." When I come in late at night, she scolds me and says, "Jewish men, in the privacy of their hearts, love shiksas—

and you, are you like all the Jews?" She remembers many
words from her parents' home. When she's in a good
mood, she stands in the living room and recites them
one by one.

This afternoon she sits at the table and pours a
glass of brandy for herself and one for me, saying, "How's
my Jew? He looks sad today."

"The Jew didn't find anything at the fair. For three
hours he looked and came away emptyhanded."

"Jews are never pleased with themselves, and
others aren't pleased with them either."

"At least you understand them."

"Because I'm one of them."

"Because of that, do people pick on you?"

"I pick on them," she says and winks. "I remind
them that Jesus was a Jew, that he was circumcised and
prayed in a synagogue."

"And what do they say?"

"They grit their teeth."

In the evening Miss Hahn makes vegetable soup
with cheese dumplings. She tells me about her childhood
and her poor parents, who saw no way out except through
the conversion of their children to Christianity. Her
young brother also converted. His conversion was more
successful. He married a rich woman and lives in the Ty-
rolean mountains. Her contact with him is slight, greet-

ing cards once or twice a year. But the hidden wound, the wound that refuses to heal, is her beloved parents. At the age of eighty-five they were sent to Auschwitz. None of the neighbors shouted in protest. When she tells me about her parents, her face changes, and old age envelops it. Once, in an instant of great concentration, she told me: "I should have left this accursed land. A land that sends old parents to the crematoria is a criminal land. It should be wiped from the face of the earth, like Sodom and Gomorrah." To distract her, I tell her about the people I have met on my way. Strange words, words I don't normally use, rise to my lips.

The next day I surveyed the fair again. Some of my rivals got there first. They, too, it seems, have learned to do the job over the years. Now it's very hard to discover an object of any value even in this neglected place. I entered Drutschik's buffet. Drutschik was as drunk as a lord and muttered in Czech. When he saw me he hugged me and called out, "Here's my man. They're all greedy scoundrels here. Only Erwin asks me for nothing. He only gives. Let everybody know that not only is the Jew smarter, he's also better. Come, let's drink to the Jews. They're worthy of great respect. They're noble people, book-loving people. They've produced distinguished doctors, writers, and publishers. I take off my hat and announce to the world that I have high regard for the Jews. I'm not afraid to express the feelings of my heart. The time has come to speak openly."

He spoke enthusiastically but looked miserable. His face was flushed and he was drooling.

"Let's sit down, Mr. Drutschik," I said.

"I won't sit down," he said. "I'll stand on my feet as long as my soul is within me."

His last words filled me with dread. I felt the place seething with an arid hostility. Outside the square was empty. A dark chill clung to the bare concrete pillars that supported the roof of the station.

"What am I doing here?" I said, and my eyes darkened. Melancholy had already attacked me here more than once, my limbs shriveling, black waves sweeping over me. I took two pills and dragged myself to my room, where I curled up in a blanket and wrapped my head in a towel. For a whole day I didn't get out of bed.

The next day Miss Hahn knocked on the door. "I brought you something to eat. You mustn't sleep without eating anything." She knows my weaknesses. When melancholy is about to drown me, she appears, reaches her hand out to me, and draws me out of the depths. She says to me, "You shouldn't be here. This place has a bad influence on you. It must be the smell of autumn, or maybe the chemical fertilizers. Go in peace and forget me." That's what she always says, but this time there was a tremor in her voice that frightened me.

CHAPTER

16

From Rondhof I continue north to Upper Rondhof. Here the leaves are already falling, and one feels the frost. The frost, I must admit, suits my body better than a moderate temperature. In the frost a somnolent part of my being comes to life. Wrapped in a coat and wearing boots, I feel more grounded.

In Upper Rondhof a Jew named Max Rauch opened a haberdashery right after the war. It has flourished and grown over the years, and now it includes six large stores, a coffee house, a restaurant, and a fine hotel. We've been friends for thirty years now. Max buys a considerable portion of my acquisitions from me. I'm glad to sell to him, because he pays a decent price and preserves the treasures with great care. Like me, he is fond of Hebrew letters, and he is proud to show me, whenever I happen to arrive, that everything he bought from me remains in good condition. Years ago I brought him a valise full of Yiddish books that I had found in a cellar in remote Schaumwasser. God knows how they made their way into that cellar. He was pleased with them, and since then I have also collected Yiddish books.

The moment I entered the region of Upper Rond-hof, I knew I had sinned: Stark's many books, the books and pamphlets he had bought with hard work and devotion, many of which I had purchased for him, had all been burned by the nuns, I had done nothing to bring them here for safekeeping in Max's large home. Now I remembered: during our last meeting, Stark had looked at his library and said with a bit of sarcasm, "I feel bad about these books, but I'm not worried. You'll find a way to circulate them." That remark wounded me deeply. I'm not a book pimp, I wanted to cry out. I drag my feet from place to place to save what can be saved. It's true I make my living from that, but it's not dishonest. The words were about to burst from my throat, but, seeing his face, the face of an abandoned man, I held my tongue. Now Stark, too, is no more.

Upper Rondhof lies on a barren, remote plateau. But since Max established the center, the place has been buzzing with peasants and tourists. People stream here from all the villages. Starting in early evening, they drink and dance in the coffee house until late at night. Soon Max will also open a movie house to attract more tourists.

With Max I feel safe and calm. Maybe it's because of the large, well-protected room on the ground floor. The room has two exits, one of them secret. All of his rooms have secret exits, he once told me. Our people must not sleep in a room without a secret exit, he said. I agree with him with all my heart. Hotel rooms make me uneasy. In them I wake up at three in the morning and struggle with insomnia until dawn. One of our kind has to sleep in a large room, with more than one door, so that he will know, even in a nightmare, that there's an escape exit.

As soon as I enter my room, I close the shutters and sink into deep sleep. Max lets me sleep as my soul desires. Sleep in his fortress is a quiet sleep, without threats, and I lose myself in it.

The next day I sit with him in the coffee house and tell him about my journeys. About the war, and about recent years, he doesn't speak much with me or anyone

else. I respect his silence, show him the books and objects, and name their price. Max is pleased with everything I bring him. Last year I brought him an antique
menorah from Alsace. He was very moved. That's how
Max is: practical wisdom and honesty mingled within
him. Only he can truly appreciate my efforts. In his spacious home he has housed all the treasures I brought him
over the years. There's a room for menorahs and sabbath
spice boxes, a room for Hebrew books, a room for Yiddish
books, and a room for other ritual objects. He bought
most of these things from me.

Sometimes it seems that my life is interred in
Max's rooms. Every year he adds a shelf. If it wasn't for
Max, it's doubtful that I would have persisted in this col-
lecting. The thought that someone is expecting you, and
that when you arrive he'll settle you in a large, comfortable room and arrange for the restaurant manager to
serve you a good meal, that thought makes my wandering
easier to bear. This time I arrive in Rondhof exhausted.
The next day I recover, sit in the coffee house, and my
body fills once again with the will to live.

Later Max leads me from room to room, showing
me the latest changes and innovations. Again I find that
everything is in its place, arranged for a long stay. But last
year an unexplained dread fell over me. For some reason
the collection seemed in danger. Max sensed my anxiety
and reassured me that everything was well guarded and

insured, and that when the time came, he would transfer all the treasures, in iron chests, to Jerusalem.

When I first met Max he was married to a tall, ambitious woman named Hermina, a woman of Danish extraction. The cold blue of the north floated in her large eyes. She hated me and the antiques Max bought from me, but I continued to come. I felt close to Max. His marriage, I was pleased to see, did not last long. Since then there has been no barrier between us. I like his practicality, his honesty, his quiet demeanor, his simple speech.

A few years ago several Jewish merchants arrived in Upper Rondhof, refugees like me. It was the sabbath. Max wanted to please them and installed a synagogue on the ground floor: three Torah scrolls that I acquired for him, a few lecterns, a holy ark, and a curtain. The merchants wrapped themselves in their prayer shawls and prayed. After the prayers, he gave them a meal. One of the merchants, whose name is Fretzl, a competitor, disclosed to me that it had been years since he had felt as close to his parents as on that sabbath. He, too, like me, wanders through these regions. But fortune does not usually favor him. That year, however, he did find a pair of silver candlesticks from the sixteenth century with the blessing for the sabbath candles engraved on their stems. But that's all. It's hard to make a living from that. He plans to emigrate to New Zealand.

A week with Max restores me to some of the hidden realms of my life. Max himself doesn't ask a lot of questions, nor does he offer advice. His appearance is surprising. Unlike most of us, he's tall, and moderation is woven into his movements. Between the counters in his shop he looks like a northerner, restrained and quiet, as if he was born not in Sadgora but in this province, where the late autumn is serene, and the colors exhilarate the soul. But at night, when I sit with him in the salon, his face changes. His forehead darkens and his gestures become agitated. He speaks simple, clear Yiddish, and an old tremor runs through it. He promises once again that everything he has purchased from me will be carefully preserved, and when the time comes, he will send it all to Jerusalem.

Sometimes, when he is in good spirits, after two or three drinks, he tells me about his ancestors, the sages of Rydzyna, about the Haggers and the Friedmans and their descendants scattered all over the world, even as far as Argentina. When he talks about his ancestors, I sense that he is connected to them by a hidden bond, though not to each of them equally. About Stark and Rollman, for example, who were also descended from Rydzyna, he hardly speaks. They grieved their forefathers too much, he once told me. Strange, this man, who is steeped in the world of action, and who looks like a local, this man becomes bent and sad when he returns to his apartment at night. You see clearly that he isn't alone. His ancestors accompany him. It's hard to know what they urge him to do. Perhaps he has become used to their reprimands and no longer responds. Once he told me that an evil worm had penetrated the renowned dynasty of Rydzyna, and that it had been gnawing at its descendants for generations. I wanted to know more, but Max wouldn't explain.

A week in his fortress renews me. The scattered links of my existence draw close together again, and I sit in the coffee house for hours. From the window I survey the spectacular orange colors of autumn. Last year I made peace with one of my rivals here, a short, affable man who admitted that he had been trailing me for years, trying in vain to learn the secret of my success. Now he had finally become a partner in a grocery store not far away. Though it's hard to compete with Max, they'll try.

Not every day brings conciliation. Sometimes melancholy takes over. My eyes darken, and I see no way out. This year I asked Max's advice, and he said, "I have put melancholy behind locks and bolts."

"All these years?"

"All these years, my dear fellow."

"And if it breaks out, what is to be done?"

"I beat it with sticks until it returns to its prison," he said, with a snicker that sent chills down my spine.

CHAPTER

17

On October first I left Max's fortress and set off on my way. The distance from here to Weinberg is about a hundred and twenty kilometers, and in Weinberg the murderer is about to move into his new home. The week in Max's company made me forget my duty. Max always wins me over. He is easygoing and generous and makes me feel like his partner in a great secret venture. In truth, he subsidizes most of my journeys. Without Max, I would have settled long ago into some gloomy grocery store, counting pennies like a beggar. He pays me in hard currency and adds to the sum here and there. When I leave his fortress, my pockets are full of marks and dollars. I know I shouldn't feel sorry for Max. He has a lot of property, and he is well protected. Still, his devotion to the collection touches my heart. It's an absolute devotion.

This year the parting was hard for me. I could have stayed another week, but I didn't dare. On the way to Weinberg I had a few obligations as well as preparations for the final struggle. As I stood in the railway station, I felt a weakening in my legs. It seemed that my life was approaching a dark alley. I suddenly felt sorry for the people who had been my hosts, especially Max, who had prepared a large, comfortable room for me. Now it seemed that he, too, was in danger.

While my thoughts grew darker, the train appeared and came to a stop. I got on as if in a dream. I went into the dining car. The waiter, who knows me, turned on the classical station.

I sat next to the window and saw Max's face in the reflection. The last evening we were in the coffee house and sipped a few drinks. I told him about Bertha and about her longings for her native city. Max confided to me that years ago he had also suffered from relentless insomnia. He was about to travel to Sadgora to prostrate himself on his ancestors' tombs to ask their forgiveness, but certain obstacles prevented him from making the journey. In the end, he never went. He fell ill, had an operation, and came through it well. Since then, his insomnia has gone away, but sharp pains sometimes awaken him at dawn. The words left his mouth softly. I saw then, for the first time, that he, too, though elegant in his dress, belonged to our family of wanderers, spending days and nights in this wasteland to drug his rebellious nerves. Still, with him, the struggle seems different. His mighty ancestors have declared war on him and caused him pain. That night he explicitly mentioned the spirits and ghosts who lie in ambush in every corner and conspire against him. The nights are especially difficult, for then their dominion is complete. He also told me about his wife, whose hatred for the Jews knew no bounds. In the first years of their marriage her hostility had a kind of defiant charm, but in the last year, she had become the incarnation of evil. She had even threatened to burn his collection.

Years ago, after a week with Max, I would board the local and ride straight to Brunhilde. But in recent years Brunhilde hasn't been what she was. Her beauty has faded and she grumbles about her two husbands, who she says cheated her out of her property. She calls the Jews soft and threatens to expose Max's dishonesty. The train passed by her house, and in my heart was neither regret nor sadness.

The train stopped at a few stations where I once liked to stay overnight. I restrained myself and didn't get off. I said to myself, maybe I'll find a devoted woman here or an antique, but that would put me off my course. I must reach Weinberg soon. But when the train stopped at Zwiren, I felt impelled to get off.

Until the middle of the last century there was a small but well-established Jewish community in Zwiren. Over the years it fell apart. The houses were abandoned, and the synagogue was deserted. But, wondrously, three houses still stand, and also the ruins of the synagogue. At the Monday fair years ago I found a ladle with the Hebrew word for milk engraved on it. Hebrew letters in these remote places move me, but my greatest discovery in Zwiren is August, a quarter-Jew. Because of that quarter he's suffered all his life, and even now people haven't stopped reminding him of his blemish. A tall, broad man, in all his gestures he resembles a peasant, the son of peasants. When he first discovered that I am a Jew, he was very pleased and invited me to his house. Since then, whenever I come to Zwiren, I stay with him. We sit and drink tea and cognac until late at night. During the war they had sent his aged mother, a half-Jew, to a camp in Germany to improve her character. She returned from

there thin and withdrawn, and she didn't speak again till
the end of her life.

When the cognac warms his heart, he speaks
about the quarter-Jew within him with a kind of secret
admiration, as if it were an aristocratic disease. With disgust he dismisses all those who have conspired against
him since his childhood. When he was a child his mother
had protected him, and his father once beat two boys who
called him names. During the war they hadn't drafted
him into a combat unit, but made him a warehouseman
in a fire company garage in southern Germany, not far
from the place where his half-Jewish mother had been
imprisoned in the camp to improve her character.

Still healthy and erect, August is now seventy-
five. In the evening we walked through the village. Again
he showed me the Jewish houses and the ruin of the synagogue. He confided that his two sons don't show much
fondness for him, and only once a year, on Christmas, do
they visit.

We sipped some more drinks. I told him about my
travels, but said nothing about Nachtigel, only hinting
that a critical year was before me. The gaiety drained
from his eyes, and sorrow settled in. Finally, he turned to
me and said in a half-serious voice, "We aren't going to
live forever. So I want to give you something of my own,
even now. This vessel, or whatever you want to call it, be-

longed to my Jewish ancestors. My mother gave it to me,
and I have kept it all these years. The truth is it has become a burden. The time has come to put it into reliable
hands."

"Why to me?" I tremble.

"Because you're a Jew, aren't you?"

"Not an observant one."

"But still a Jew."

I removed the wrapping and saw a kiddush cup
engraved with the words "Holy Sabbath." I wrapped it in
its velvet cloth again. I wanted to say, I don't have a house
of my own, where shall I put it? But I was too moved to
speak. He looked at me like a peasant who had sold his
faithful animal to a cattle trader.

"Why are you giving me this now?"

"I don't want to keep it in my house. That's all."
He raised his voice a little. I lowered my head. "You understand," he said. "I can't keep it any longer."

"Then I'll watch over it," I said softly.

"I've done my part. It's no longer my responsibility, thank God."

"I'll watch over it," I repeated, wanting to flee.

The train came early, and I left him hastily, as if
the earth were burning under my feet.

18

From Zwiren to Upper Zwiren is only half an hour by
train. But the atmosphere is entirely different. Upper
Zwiren lies on an exposed plateau that rises far from
neighboring settlements, and if the train didn't pass by at
its feet, it is doubtful whether anyone would remember
its existence. I discovered it many years ago, and since
then I never skip it. The train arrives around noon. Few

passengers get on or off. The station says more about the place than anything: a derelict structure without bathrooms or supervisor, it resembles an abandoned chapel.

This time the wind was cold, as before a snowfall, but the climb wasn't difficult. I carried my valise with vigor, and at one o'clock I was in my usual place, under a broad-limbed oak with a view of the surroundings. I took out the sandwiches and thermos that August had prepared for me. The sandwiches he makes have a homey taste, maybe because of the fresh cream cheese. His coffee is thick and warms the entire body. August himself was as a hidden presence this time. I took from my valise the kiddush cup he'd given me. It was a simple goblet, undecorated, and the letters engraved on it were crude, without polish.

Sometimes August could be amused by the quarter-Jew within him. If he said something clever, he would announce, "It wasn't me, it was the quarter in me." Other times he would talk about the quarter as if it were a childhood disease that had long been cured. Only when he spoke about his mother and her many years of muteness did his blue eyes fill with tears. Years ago, when I told him that I intended to travel to Jerusalem one day, he asked with the earnestness of a peasant, "Is it so you can visit the Church of the Holy Sepulchre?"

"August," I said. "I am a Jew."

"I forgot," he said. "I should have remembered."
Then he asked, "The Jews don't believe in the reincarnation of Jesus?"

"No."

"What do they believe in?"

"In the Old Testament."

"And the Old Testament doesn't mention Jesus?"

"No."

"If so, what did the priest mean in his sermon on Sunday?"

August's questions exhude the smells of the earth. His forefathers were peasants, and from them he inherited innocence and strength. When he recalls his father, who worked his farm with his own hands, no trace of the Jew is visible in him. Sometimes I love the peasant in him more than the frayed quarter. The Jewish quarter in him makes him look sad. Sadness does not suit his round face.

Before melancholy overcame me, I remembered the purpose of my arrival here. I drew the pistol from my valise and unwrapped it. That solid piece of metal always pleases me. In the end I sell the treasures and manuscripts, but it remains faithful to me. Only Max knows the secret and supplies me with a few new magazines of cartridges every time we meet.

After I fired two magazines, I heard a voice calling. The voice was clear and strong, and I bent to listen.

When the voice called again, it sounded like Bertha's voice. Years ago I brought her here to show her the landscape and the pistol. At first she was excited, but this soon turned to dread. She murmured words I could not understand, and I was forced to return her to the station, to console her. Needless to say, I never got to show her the gun. I didn't know then what forces lay within her. Now Bertha is sitting on the riverbank staring at the water. God only knows what thoughts she harbors.

I cleaned the gun. Every time I clean it, I feel myself fill with patience, and the fear of death diminishes. Once Max told me that the transition to the next world must be very short. When I asked him how it is done, he replied, "It takes practice."

When I wrapped up the pistol, I saw Bertha once more, the way she had first appeared to me: a young woman immersed in her work, her expression intense, as if her gaze were fixed on some wondrous sight. Wonder gave her face the beauty of someone who heeds her own mysteries.

It was four o'clock. The sun was already setting, kissing the horizon. I returned the pistol to my valise and hurried back down. At five the last local passes through, and I did not want to miss it. Strange, after every target practice here, I see many faces. All the stations bunch together and acquaintances who live many kilometers apart, Jews, half-Jews, and enemies, mingle with each other, like relatives. That vision belongs to this place alone. This time, too, it was revealed to me. But this time, for some reason, the people were burdened with bundles and sunk into themselves, as if they knew there was no escape.

From here I know I should have gone straight to Weinberg. But I dreaded the thought that I was approaching
the murderer. I wanted to see Rabbi Zimmel. Over the
years I have spent many days in his company. The journey without his blessing now seemed like a disaster. I got
off at Sandberg.

The station in Sandberg is like all the other small
stations. The square is gray concrete, and the buffet is

cramped. Rabbi Zimmel always sits with me until the train comes and then sees me off. Waiting in this deserted place has often been an hour of grace for me.

I was barely off the train when I knew something was wrong. The buffet's only window was shut tight, and a sharp light flooded the square. Tethered horses were pulled from the rear cars. The horses advanced with short steps, flinching, as if they had been commanded to walk on coals.

I entered the buffet and asked to see the owner. He told me Rabbi Zimmel was very sick and no longer left his room.

"Since when, my dear fellow?" I asked the gentile like a fool.

"I don't know," he said in a dumb, arrogant tone.

"And where is the carriage?"

"At this hour there is no carriage. The driver has gone back to his village." He turned away. I stood in the illuminated square and saw the tethered horses standing at the entrance to the storehouses. Their heads were bent and vapor streamed from their nostrils, as if they had climbed a mountain. On the spot I decided: though the valise was heavy, I would walk.

Until the end of the last century there was still a Jewish community in Sandberg. Over the years the young people moved to cities, and the old people departed one by one. Rabbi Zimmel, who was then young, remained to watch over the few old people, the synagogue, and its extensive library. During the war he was sent to the camps with the old people. First he was deported to Minsk, and then sent to labor camps. From there he was taken to a small extermination camp in Hungary. At the last minute he was saved. When he returned to Sandberg after the war, he was astonished to find the synagogue secured with the very lock he had placed there. The key was still in its niche. He had intended to come for a single day, to prostrate himself on his ancestors' tombs, and then to join the refugees on their way to Palestine. But when he found everything in its place, he took pity on the synagogue and its books. So he stayed. It turned out that a woman who had worked for the Jews for many years had come every week and cleaned the synagogue and the adjoining rooms. Several times vandals had been about to set the place on fire, but the woman had threatened them with divine retribution, and they were deterred. She died a few days before his arrival.

Since his return, Rabbi Zimmel has not left the place. If a wandering Jew finds his way there, he feeds him, lodges him in one of his rooms, and shows him the many books in the library. I first arrived there in 1952, confused, weary, and lost.

I hurried to reach him before dark.

It's good that you came, he told me with his eyes, from which a faint light glimmered. I sat next to his bed and tried to hear. With his eyes he gestured toward a letter on the table. Among other things, it said: In the adjoining room are iron boxes. Put the books in them and send them to Jerusalem.

To overcome my fear I revealed to him that I intended to go to Weinberg to take the life of the murderer. What would happen after that was not important. Hearing those words, his eyes opened wide. It was evident from them that he had caught something of my meaning. It was important that Rabbi Zimmel know I had not shirked my duty.

The doctor entered, and I retired to the next room. The doctor asked no questions of his patient, and the patient did not complain. That silence glued me to the wall. When the doctor left I asked, "How is the Rabbi?" He bowed his head and said, "God is our savior." I wanted to chide him. A doctor is not a rabbi. From him we expect practical words. I restrained myself. The doctor went out into the darkness as I watched.

When I entered his room, Rabbi Zimmel's eyes were open. I told him about Max and August, and asked him not to worry, because Max's hand was open and generous, and the place remained dear to him. The rabbi apparently absorbed what I said, and a smile played on his lips.

THE IRON TRACKS

I went out and lit the candelabrum in the synagogue. When I was a child, Grandfather wanted to attract
me to prayer but didn't know how. Grandmother would
read the prayers with me, and I was certain that only
women knew how to pray. For many days I sat here and
read with Rabbi Zimmel. His way of reading was marvelous, as if he were touching a fruit and smelling its
perfume. We read the Bible, Mishnah, and Midrash.

All these years Rabbi Zimmel sat and wrote the
history of the place and of the Zimmel family, which
hadn't left Sandberg for about seven hundred years. His
forefathers had written many books: about Jewish law,
ethics, Biblical exegesis, and Kabbalah. A person could
spend his entire life here and manage to study only a few
of the treasures they had left behind.

It was a few years ago, when he had finished list-
ing the books and preparing a full bibliography, that he
decided to pack them up and send them to Jerusalem. But
he was prevented from doing so from on high. First he
fell ill, and when he got well, nightmares disturbed his
sleep. His ancestors were not pleased with his decision.
He struggled with them in his sleep, and in the end they
prevailed: he did not ship the books to Jerusalem, nor did
he himself go there.

It was hard to make him talk about that, but about
other things he would willingly speak. In the beginning of
the previous century about twenty Jewish families had

lived here. Their solid stone houses still stand. On our nightly walks he told me many things about them, a marvelous group of merchants and sages. Mobs sometimes attacked them and drove them out, but they would return and rebuild the ruins. Now smoke rose from the houses; the peasants were eating supper, and a dense tranquility hung like mist over the meadows, as if this were how it had always been.

I telephoned Max and asked him to come. His devotion to Rabbi Zimmel was complete. Whenever he had a free hour, he came here and brought fruit, vegetables, and dairy products. Like his ancestors, Rabbi Zimmel was a vegetarian.

Meanwhile, the rabbi beckoned me. I approached his bed. He gestured toward the iron chests with his eyes, and I promised him that I would pack the books. Together with Max, I would send them to Jerusalem.

Then Max arrived. A new light shone in Rabbi Zimmel's eyes. The three of us sat in silence. Suddenly Max turned to me and asked, "Did you practice?"

"I shot two magazines," I answered, surprised by his question.

"You should practice every month." He spoke in a language not his own.

"I don't have many chances."

"You must."

He had never spoken to me like that before. I wanted to turn to him and say, Dear brother, why are you pressing me in this difficult hour? He looked at me angrily and said, "I practice once a week."

That very night Rabbi Zimmel died. Max wept, and I didn't know how to console him. Words that weren't my own arose within me, and I said, "Rabbi Zimmel has completed his task in this world, and now he has been gathered unto his ancestors. His life was clear and unstained." Max didn't respond to my words. His face darkened, and his forehead became clouded. We buried Rabbi Zimmel in the cemetery next to his forefathers, and together we recited, "God, full of mercy." Then we sat in the buffet and drank stale coffee.

I thought of telling him about Nachtigel, but I restrained myself. I felt that I must perform that duty without asking help from anyone. Max's expression was frightening. Large furrows settled into his face and deepened, and his lower lip trembled. Suddenly he got up and said loudly, "I must go home." I wanted to detain him, but he was determined.

CHAPTER

20

Dizzy and empty, I boarded the night local and set out on my way. Across from me sat a short, clumsy woman with a blank smile on her lips. I told her that a few hours before I had buried a man very close to me. Upon hearing my words, her smile twisted. She covered her mouth with her right hand.

"Where?" she asked in obvious surprise.

"Here," I said, and I saw before my eyes the two robust peasants who dug the grave, and Max standing there wearing a yarmulke, pressing the prayer book to his breast with both hands. After the burial we walked through the harvested fields. No one was there. We crossed the brook and stood in a deserted clearing surrounded by leafless trees. Max looked taller than usual. His head was slightly bent, and his mouth was open, as if he had just realized that life passes and people dear to us depart in untimely fashion, that remaining behind is difficult and meaningless.

"Sandberg is cursed," said the woman in a clear, unpleasant voice.

"Were you hurt there, too?"

"I will never go to Sandberg again."

"Why?"

"Because everyone there hates me." She had the growl of an animal that has escaped from its cage. Her open, cloudy eyes were flooded with fear, and it was clear that just a short time ago she had been within the reach of her pursuers.

"Do you have family there?" I ask.

"I have three sisters, three witches, who make me miserable."

"What do they want from you?"

"For me to get married. I don't want to get married. I want to live as I please, without a husband and children."

"That's understandable."

"But not to my pious sisters. They're sure I'm a loose woman. I'm not. I'm just looking for some peace, nothing more." In the past women like her would fall right into my arms. A woman in flight has no complaints. She's submissive and devoted and asks only for a little affection, a sandwich, and travel money. After the night, you forget her easily. As for the one sitting before me, the pathetic quarrel with her sisters gave her face the look of an abandoned animal. Her stubby fingers, which looked cut off, covered her mouth repeatedly.

"You don't have to get married," I told her.

"It's too bad my sisters can't hear you." The words left her mouth heavily and crudely.

"I'm prepared to say it to them."

Hearing those words, she whimpered, "No one understands me. They hunt me down like a rabbit. I'm not a rabbit." Her disheveled face expressed foolishness and pain, and she repeated, "I'm not a rabbit, I don't want to be hunted."

I talked to her the way I talk with all women, with words that have a hint of flattery and a pinch of pretense. I even told her she was pretty. The words did their work. She wiped the tears from her face and her peasant features were revealed in all their coarseness.

"What are you doing here?" she asked.

"I'm a peddler."

She apparently didn't catch the meaning of the word and said, "It's good you weren't born in that accursed place. They'll pursue me the rest of my life."

"In a year or two your sisters will get old and leave you alone."

"Are you sure?"

"I'm positive."

She bowed her head as if she were about to kneel. I chided her, "You mustn't kneel. Life is hard, but you've got to stand straight. Standing straight is what makes us human beings." She was startled and apologized.

I remembered Max again. The words he had spoken seeped into me, and only now did I feel their sting. Nor had his departure been ordinary. He hadn't said, Come back to me soon, as he used to, but "I've got to go." As if he'd been summoned to someplace unpleasant. I wanted to call out, Don't go, sit with me until the fury passes. But for some reason it felt wrong to detain him, and I let him go.

When we neared Steinberg, I got to my feet and said, "I must get off here."

"Are you leaving me?" She opened her expressionless eyes.

"I have to get off. There are things that a man has to do, and soon."

"Too bad," she said, frightened.

I took off my wristwatch and said, "Allow me to give you this watch. It isn't expensive, but it brings good luck." She took the watch and began to kiss my hands wildly, as if to show me what her mouth could do in a moment of passion.

21

I reached Steinberg toward evening. The distance from
Steinberg to the murderer's house is forty kilometers. I
got off here because I wanted to build up some courage, to
rest, and to remember a sight that had slipped from my
memory. I got off without emotion and went into the buffet. I have learned that hidden things are often revealed
in strange and neglected places. I had two drinks and immediately saw Rabbi Zimmel's face. During the past two

years he had been completely absorbed in preserving and rebinding his books. He studied just an hour or two a day, and devoted the rest of his strength to his labors. He did the work quietly and with great precision.

The buffet emptied, and I set off on my way. I have a few secret lodgings in the area, where, in the past, I used to hide out and sleep for a few days without interruption. A lot of snow can fall in this season, but this year there has only been frost. In this remote place I picked up the murderer's trail. Here, a few years ago, in a wretched inn called "Schneeweiss," a group of retired officers held a memorial party. I could see them from my room, strutting about and calling one another not by name but by rank. Then I heard Nachtigel's name for the first time.

At first the landlady looked askance at me, but when she saw that I read newspapers, she changed her mind. She told me that her husband had fallen as a hero in the East, and her two sons had been drafted a few months before the end of the war and had perished in bombings. Since then, whenever I return here, she tells me the same story. Her pain seems to have faded by now, but she continues to repeat the story obsessively. Five years ago I brought a woman here with me, not a very pretty one, whom I found on the train. After that the landlady stopped speaking to me. Last year I couldn't restrain myself, and I said to her, "If my presence disturbs you, I won't come anymore."

"I didn't mean that," she said and burst into tears.
"Then what is it?"

"It's hard for me to bear having a prostitute in the house."

"She wasn't a prostitute. She was a widow." I raised my voice.

"Pardon me," she said, and shrank behind the counter.

After that she no longer said "prostitutes," but "certain women," and she was pleased with herself for having outwitted me. It's hard for me to bear her muttering, and more than once I've been tempted to skip her inn, but the thought of the broad bed, the high window covered with an embroidered curtain, the two landscapes hanging above the bed, make me change my mind. The room infuses me with the desire for deep slumber. I sleep without interruption, getting up only for meals.

This time, when she saw that I had come alone, she was obviously pleased and said, "The room is waiting for you, sir." Without delay, without becoming tangled in her words, I went upstairs. The room was just as I had left it a year ago. The bed, the writing table, the armchair. I was moved at the sight of these orderly, mute objects, which looked as if they expected me.

At dinner a retired railroad conductor sat next to me. He downed a few drinks and subsided into nostalgia. He spoke of the days when he was a young soldier, fighting on the Eastern Front, of the cold, of enjoying a good meal, and of feeling that he was bringing salvation to the world.

"How?" I wondered.

"We killed Jews. It was dreadful work, but very necessary. Work that brought relief to the soul. True, at first you were repelled by the screams, but little by little you learned that you were doing something important."

"Not all of them were killed."

"You're wrong. We went from village to village and from hiding place to hiding place. We didn't leave a trace. That was an exhausting mission, a dirty mission, but we did our duty to the end."

He also told me that when he was captured by the Russians, he learned that his wife, whom he loved, and to whom he was devoted, had not been faithful to him during the war. She had slept with old men and boys and shamelessly violated the sanctity of their marriage. Fortunately, he was a prisoner for only a short time. He returned to the village and killed her without hesitation. In the village they were sure the Russians had done it. "Why contradict them?" he said coarsely. "The main thing is that she was killed, right? An unfaithful woman deserves a violent death. A violent death befits her." A yellow glow flooded his ruddy face.

CHAPTER

22

The next morning I rose early and continued on my journey. I knew that I had to make my way to Weinberg on foot
and on my own. The morning was gray. Light snowflakes
fell on the hills but did not stick. I had made this trip
more than once. Here, I had bought books and treasures.
I had met people and rested in pensions. In the winter
months I would drag from village to village as if in night-

marish sleep. This time it was different: as if a yoke had been removed from me.

Near a tall tree I saw my mother sitting in an old armchair, a cigarette in her mouth, examining me with a questioning gaze. What will become of you? Your reading is faulty, and your writing is full of mistakes. Unlike my father, she believed that a person must study the great books well. My refusal to attend school hurt her. In those years I was drawn to Father, to his adventures and visions. Night after night I would sit and watch the small bands he would send from his hiding place to set fire to forests and factories. The arsonists, upon returning from their missions, would be covered with dust. Their eye sockets would be black, and malicious joy would sparkle in their gaze. Thus Father sought to release the region from its suffering.

Mother did not take part in party activities after the assassination. Were it not for some friends from her youth, she would have sunk into total isolation. Most of the time she sat and read. I was unable to appreciate her nobility. I was sure that she was wasting her time on nothing, avenging herself on Father. I was sure that she no longer believed in reforming society. Her silence stifled me. I would flee the house, roam the streets, and take up with Ruthenian boys. More than once I returned home wounded and bleeding. Mother would care for me quietly and patiently, as if I weren't her rebellious son but a creature to be pitied. When Father came to take me, I didn't kiss her on the forehead but ran to him, as if fleeing an oppressive place.

During the war the Ruthenians drove him from his hiding place. He was forced outdoors in a short, tattered coat, blinded by the daylight. For weeks we wandered through the fields, seeking the charity of his friends. Everyone shunned him or refused to open the door. At night we would sleep in barns or abandoned pens. Father blamed no one, nor did he make excuses.

After years in dark hiding places, he relished being in the sunlight again. Sometimes we would stop near a stream and doze. When he awoke there was a tremor in the muscles of his face. A sudden smile would rise on his lips; then immediately they would contort. Not even those grimaces contained reproach or anger. He made a few familiar gestures as if to say, I was mistaken, I miscalculated. Then he stopped that too. He was too preoccupied with himself to speak with me, and I walked by his side without disturbing his thoughts.

One morning a truck drove up and two Germans seized us. They forced us onto the truck, kicking and beating us. "That's that," Father said, as if relieved. I was fifteen. I saw for the first time that he was a head shorter than I.

Thus we arrived in Nachtigel's camp. It was a small, brutal labor camp, where people died from cold and hard work. To our surprise we found Mother there. She was wearing a long dress and a thick sweater, and clods of mud clung to her boots. She was glad to see us and spoke to us both. She said it was especially tough for Communists there. Everyone avoided them, picked on them, and reminded them of their deeds. The Germans and Ukrainians beat people without making distinctions. Nachtigel executed people daily. I, it turned out, was stronger than my parents.

I worked, loading coal like a trained laborer. Father, too, worked at this, without falling behind. His companions in hard labor didn't forget his past. At every opportunity they would remind him that he was a fanatic, that he had joined the Ruthenians and would send them into the Jewish streets to steal and loot. Father didn't reply. One morning Nachtigel shot him because he came late to the lineup. Mother worked in the sewing shop, and at night she would bring me pieces of bread at great risk. I asked her not to do it, but she wouldn't listen. One night she, too, was shot, near the fence.

CHAPTER

23

I headed south, away from the iron tracks. In the past I would hire a wagon, ride down to Little Steinberg, and stay there for a few days. In Little Steinberg I once found a few rare books that Rabbi Zimmel had declared to be treasures. Once I brought Bertha here during the summer to show her the broad cornfields. She was moved. She spoke in a rush about her life of wandering, about how she could find no peace because she had been wrenched from her beloved home. The sight of her charmed me and I couldn't grasp the pain in her words. I was sure her distress was momentary, but she went on with mounting pathos until it rang in my ears. Finally I stopped believing her. It seemed that she was putting herself into a kind of self-enchantment, blinding herself with illusions. I chided her: "We don't need a house of our own, or a river of our own. We must live without illusions and within ourselves." She listened to me and fell silent. That evening her eyes were swollen, and she didn't mention Zalishtshik anymore.

The next day, when I accompanied her to the train, I realized that I had been foolish and asked her forgiveness. "Why are you begging my pardon?" she said. "My weakness deserves a good scolding. One mustn't yearn for a city that murdered its sons and daughters. I have to wrench such yearnings from my heart and accept that I no longer have a permanent place in the world." Her words seared me.

In the evening in the Black Horse Tavern I met Kron, Father's good friend. He had aged. His face was like those of the old peasants sitting at the table with him. He didn't recognize me.

"I'm Siegelbaum's son," I said to him.

"Which Siegelbaum?"

"From the party."

"The party?" He was surprised and closed his eyes.

"We used to meet on May Day at Stark's," I tried to remind him.

He made a dismissive motion with his hand, without opening his eyes. But when I mentioned Rollman, he opened them, and I saw that the name had rekindled his extinguished memory.

I invited him to have a drink. At one time Kron wanted to emigrate to Australia. But he apparently never left this region, and here he fell into decline. After two drinks he began to talk about Rollman and Stark and Father, and their youth in the training camps, where they were toughened for the ordeals to come. About the war and the estrangement of the Ruthenians he didn't speak. Suddenly, he clutched his head and fell silent. That night I learned that they had intended to send Mother to Moscow to prepare her for a senior post in the party. But someone, Kron revealed to me, had blackballed that loyal woman.

Later, he remembered them all one by one. Rollman was our senior member, he did more for the party than anyone else in the region. His leadership extended over Bucovina and Galicia, reaching as far as Poland. Only Stark, his secret rival, reached such a high rank.

Kron called Father a hero who knew how to conscript troops, and who, like Trotsky in his time, could inspire them and ease their fear of death. He also spoke of himself, but without vanity. He blamed his religious education, which he said deadened his imagination and his ambition to do great deeds. And he blamed his father, who used to force him to study ancient books night and day, moldy old books that had nothing to do with reality. When he spoke of his youth, his memory was clear, but he had forgotten the name of his beloved mother, for some reason.

"Where are you headed now?" he asked me in a youthful voice.

"I'm returning to the south."

"It's good that you're returning."

"The south is no different from the north." Something in me wanted to tell him the truth.

"It is different, my dear fellow, it is different." Now it was clear that he was immersed in a different geography.

He asked no more questions but continued talking. He spoke of the devotion of the few, who had abandoned old parents and set out on long journeys to redeem the world. At first the Ruthenians loved them and were proud of them, but at the time of crisis they abandoned them, leaving them to their own devices. The Ruthenians themselves joined the murderers. He delivered his speech in a quiet voice, as if reading from a book.

Despair, it seemed, had not marked him even now. He told me plainly that he could no longer afford to keep a room, but he had two strong backpacks. He kept food in one and clothes in the other. During most of the spring and summer he slept in barns, and in winter the taverns were open until late at night, sometimes until dawn. At dawn, he would light a small fire and make a cup of coffee for himself.

I wanted to give him my winter coat, but he refused. "It's not right for someone of my age to accept gifts. A man of eighty-three has few needs, and the main thing is not to exploit one's fellow man. Isn't that so?"

CHAPTER

24

After midnight I boarded a train, curled up next to the window, and wept. It had been years since I cried. It seemed to me that Kron was standing in the darkness and waving goodbye. Like my father, he had the hands of a worker. The empty coach and the rhythmic motion did not calm my nerves. Tears flowed from my eyes as if from a leaky vessel. It's strange how self-pity strikes just when it seems to have been subdued.

The Iron Tracks

I had two drinks, lit a cigarette, and watched the darkness falling on the leafless trees and the light growing on the horizon. A thin layer of snow covered the mountains, and a sparse, morning mist rose over the small stone houses. Now I can get off, I said to myself, and I got off.

Years ago I used to meet Gobias the wagon driver in the square in front of this station. He was a tall, laconic man who, without asking questions or even speaking, would bring me to Upper Steinberg. I greatly appreciated his silence, and never violated the constraint he imposed upon himself. Now I was glad the wagon wasn't waiting in its place. I could make my way on foot.

According to my calculations, the train put me slightly off the main route, but that made the distance to Weinberg even shorter. From here it is twenty-four kilometers. If I am determined, I can make my way in two days. The area is hardly inhabited. A few houses are scattered on the hills, and aside from the tavern, there's no temptation. In the past I liked to sit there, sip drinks, and look at the peasant women's faces. The women's drinking customs are different from the men's. First they chat, joke, and curse. After a few drinks, a kind of bitterness falls upon them, and they withdraw into the corners and curl up like sick animals. Only when the men come in after work do they wake up and flee to their homes.

In winter, latent hatred of the Jews arises here of its own accord. A single word is enough to rekindle the blaze. In the past the curses would frighten or infuriate me. But in recent years I have liked sitting and watching the people. Once a dispute broke out here over the number of Jews in the world. Some contended that most of them had been exterminated, and only a ghost or goblin remained here and there. But the others claimed that there were many Jews, and they multiplied fast. Now they were to be found wherever there was power and money.

The owner of the tavern was pleased to see me and immediately offered me a drink and a sandwich. He calls me the man from Hungary, and for some reason he is convinced that I am planning to build a brick factory here. He told me at length what had happened in the area during the past year. Among other things he reported that in June a big party had been held in the tavern courtyard in honor of the sixtieth anniversary of the founding of the Steinberg Regiment. All the veterans of the regiment had gathered, the widows, sons, and grandsons. There was even a small orchestra. The celebration lasted all night.

"And who gave the speech?" I tried to draw him out.

"Colonel Nachtigel."

Whenever I hear Nachtigel's name, my arms go limp, and I am afraid I won't be up to doing the deed. I feel the same weakness in my nightmares. I want to overcome it by the hike I'm taking to Weinberg.

"Man is an insect," I blurted out.

The tavern owner widened his eyes and then narrowed them purposely, saying, "I agree with you. Every tavern owner would agree with you. Night after night they wallow on the floor like pigs. I have to throw them out by myself. Once they're outside, in the cold, they wake up and crawl home on all fours. That's how it is, night after night."

"And can't anything improve them?"

"Man's a monster, don't you know that?"

That coarse sentence summons up for me, out of nowhere, my father's face. Father used to say, "Conditions corrupt, exploitation corrupts. Remove those obstacles, and man will be revealed to you in all his glory." Even in the labor camp, bent over and reviled, he did not repudiate his faith. Once when he said, "Not even in hell will I deny my faith in man," one of the prisoners, a ruffian, approached him and slapped him in the face to remind him that the Communists had burned down his cement block factory.

CHAPTER

25

I stayed at the tavern for about two hours and then set out. Snow was falling, and the cold grew more intense. But I was determined to make my way on foot. Murder is no trivial matter, and I must become fit. I progressed about two kilometers into the woods and unwrapped the pistol. I set up a target and fired a magazine. The reports were loud, and I aimed well. The accurate shots pleased me.

THE IRON TRACKS

At this point my annual trip reaches the three-quarter mark, and here I usually permit myself to tarry a bit, to eat a good meal, and to plan the last quarter. This time a new spirit throbbed within me, as if I knew I wouldn't be back here again.

According to the information in my possession, Nachtigel is now seventy-two. He was married but had no children. During the war his wife was responsible for sending warm clothing to the front. Nachtigel returned home from Lvov several times on leave. He didn't bring his wife to the East. He began his career in Bucovina, transferred to Galicia, and finished his service in Poland. In all of those places he was responsible for labor camps. He killed the weak and inefficient. He would keep the strong and those with professional skills under his supervision for some time, beating them and torturing them until they weakened and died, then others would be sent in their place. For his efficiency and devotion he was promoted and received several medals.

After the war he escaped to Uruguay and lived there among other former officers. In 1968, he returned and settled in the Zwiren region. From time to time he would change houses. Three houses were at his disposal: one was his and he inherited the other two. At first he hired sentries, former soldiers of his, to guard his dwelling. After his wife died, he wasn't afraid anymore.

He settled in Steinberg and finally bought a new house in the region of his childhood, in beautiful Weinberg.

The sky was low and dark, and the snow kept falling. I felt that if I continued walking, my legs would freeze, and I would never reach Weinberg. I boarded the local that everybody calls "the little train" and curled up near a window.

The trip and the tension had exhausted me, and I closed my eyes. Again I was with my father, dragged from hut to hut, completely submerged in the Ruthenian language. Ruthenian words summon up before my eyes the straw mattresses upon which my father used to lay me down at night. It has been years since a Ruthenian word has left my mouth, but that language is still woven into my being. All the dairy dishes, the breads, the drinks—they all come to life at the sound of a single word. Nor do I forget in my sleep how the Ruthenians trampled on my father's devotion. Nevertheless, in my sleep everything is different. Even a hostile word pleases me. I'm with Father again, as if we had never been separated.

I awoke in a panic and went to the dining car. In this season it is often crammed with drunks. They wallow in their hallucinations and invoke the memory of their army days, when they ate out of cans and swept through the Russian steppes on motorcycles to conquer the world. But this time the dining car was empty. The owner lost both his legs during the war. He offered me a sandwich.

After making the sandwich, he sat down next to me. During the war he served in Czernowitz for some time, moved on to Galicia, and finished his service in Poland. At the end of the war he tried to escape from a prison camp, but the cold was fierce, his legs froze, and he developed gangrene. Had it not been for an old Ukrainian woman who took him to the hospital, he probably would have died. I ask him if he happened to run into Nachtigel on his way. To my surprise he disclosed many details about him to me. He had been under Nachtigel's command for some time and had seen him at work: he was a professional.

"What made him a professional?" I asked.

"His faith that the extermination of Jews would bring relief to the world," he answered, short and swift.

"You also believed."

"Certainly. Without belief, you don't kill." His blue eyes looked directly at me. There is no regret in his heart. On the contrary, the years and the suffering have only intensified his faith. I overcame my muteness and raised my voice: "It is forbidden to kill."

"That's true, but we had to kill the Jews."

If he weren't a cripple, I would have taken him by the throat and throttled him. There was no one in the dining car, just the two of us, but his proximity paralyzed me. Still, I got my tongue to work and shouted, "No excuses, murderer!"

"I'm not making an excuse. I'm going right to the point. Extermination of the Jews was a great task, a historical mission. No one could have overcome them. They controlled everything. Only the Germans, in partnership with the Austrians, could bring it off. Clear thinking was necessary, thinking without fear, without hesitation, and with great precision."

"Shut your mouth!" I grabbed his throat.

"My legs have been amputated. I have no choice but to obey your instructions."

"You're a murderer!"

"I'm not a murderer. I did what I was told."

I punched his face. He was scared but didn't call for help. His face became rigid.

"No politeness!" I told him. "For killers there is no politeness."

"I'm not asking for mercy," he stammered. "I hate mercy."

"I didn't beat you for what you did in the past. For that I should kill you. I beat you for your thoughts now. If I were braver, if I had something of you in me, I wouldn't hesitate to butcher you."

He didn't reply, and I kept on shouting and threatening. But the more I shouted, the slacker my hands grew, and weakness seeped into me. Finding no other words to say, I called him a murderer again, a bloody murderer. The words came out of my mouth soundlessly, drowned out by the deafening noise of the wheels. When the train reached the station, I stepped to the door, and from there I threatened: "There's no forgiveness, not even for cripples." I got off the train and walked away hurriedly.

Only at a distance from the iron tracks did I feel how awkward my words had been. As after every failure, this time, too, I felt physically unclean: A greasy odor rose from my clothing, and my face was unshaven. I paused. This was the way to Weinberg, I knew it well. It was hard to go wrong: tall oaks grew along the road, sheltering the low houses. Still, it seemed to me that I hadn't gotten here under my own power, but that a kind of nightmare had propelled me from tunnel to tunnel, through long railway cars, ugly buffets, and iron-barred caves, where tethered horses stood with frightening patience.

CHAPTER

26

From here to Weinberg is a distance of two and a half kilometers. But before going up to the village, I must visit Lotte, Rabbi Zimmel's cousin. After the war she returned to her native village and found that the cemetery had been broken into. The tombstones had been desecrated, and weeds covered the graves. She immediately rented a small house near the cemetery and be-

gan to restore it. Like her elderly cousin, she never again
left the village.

Over the years her face changed, and now her fig-
ure is like a local peasant woman's, short and sturdy. Her
brow is tan, and talk is hard for her. When I appear at the
door, she steps backward and an awkward smile spreads
over her face.

"How are you, Lotte?"

"Fine," she said, her smile becoming more awkward.

"It's very cold in Steinberg."

"It's cold here, too."

That's about how our conversations usually begin
and end. It's hard to draw a word out of her. Sometimes
when I ask, she shows me the cemetery, which is full of
flowers now and looks like an exotic garden. But, she
surprised me this time.

"How is my cousin?"

This caught me short, but I recovered quickly and
lied, "Excellent."

"Can I offer you a cup of tea?"

"Gladly."

She stepped away to prepare the tea, and I surveyed the house. It was an old peasant house whose low
ceiling and thick beams grazed your head. The building
was no more than a square room with an old brick oven in

the middle. Some distance from the oven are a wooden table and two benches. At one side, an old dresser. These appear to be all her possessions.

In the past she would tell me about her garden, about the cow, Lily, about her good nature and the fine milk she produced. If I happened to come at the end of the summer, she would make a little package of cucumbers and tomatoes for me. Over the years her words had grown scarcer. Her contact with people, which was limited in any event, became even more restricted.

She served me the cup of tea. "Thank you very much," I said, but she didn't respond. I saw my presence wasn't easy for her. She sat across from me, shrunken, without uttering a word. If she weren't so closed, I would tell her about her elderly cousin's death. It's hard for me to know how to deal with heavy-tongued people. I was afraid of a sudden outburst and didn't reveal a thing to her. Fortunately, she didn't ask again, and I was glad.

A year ago she complained to me that hooligans had broken through the fence and desecrated the tombstones. She spoke with great anger, and it was clear that if a trespasser had found his way onto her land, she would not have hesitated to raise an axe against him.

"How are the neighbors this year?" I asked cautiously.

"Fine," she said. She was sixty-six at that time, but her body didn't show it. Her legs stood firm on the ground.

Afterward, as if beside the point, she told me that Lily had gotten sick that spring. She had lain down in her stall and refused to get up. Lotte feared for the cow's life and called for the veterinarian. He came and examined Lily and announced that she had caught a fatal and contagious disease. She had to be destroyed immediately; he would summon the inspectors. Lotte pleaded with him, but in vain. Lily died that night. The next day, when the inspectors came to kill her, they only found the body.

"That's a miracle, isn't it?" The awkward smile returned to her face.

"True," I said absently.

"If they had come to shoot her, I wouldn't have let them. An animal should die in the place where it was used to living. You mustn't shoot animals." Her voice quivered.

"You're right."

"The veterinarians are cruel people. You shouldn't do what they tell you," she said and burst into tears.

I wanted to console her and said, "A miracle happened for Lily. She died in peace and without unnecessary suffering."

"She did suffer. She suffered a lot."

"But she wasn't put to death by evil people."

"You're right. But we were companions for many years. It's hard for me to live without her. In the summer we used to go out to pasture together." Amazement spread over her face as if she had grasped something that had evaded her all the years. Her mouth suddenly shut, and she didn't add a word. Her face was covered with the same blank awkwardness that had greeted me on my arrival at her house.

CHAPTER

27

I reached Weinberg toward evening. I was tired and my
arms felt slack. I went to the kiosk and asked for lemon
soda. The sweet liquid dispelled the weakness slightly,
but not the dizziness. The sights of the past few days and
the visit to Lotte still clung to me. For a minute I imagined that the legless buffet owner whom I punched in the
face was coming after me on his crutches. Lotte hadn't

accompanied me to the door. I said goodbye to her, and she didn't reply.

I stood near the kiosk and watched the customers' movements. They were elderly people, their moderate gait filled with rural tranquility. I knew Weinberg well. It seemed unusually quiet to me. Then I remembered that after the Tuesday fair, they remove the boards, collect the trash, and on two high wagons hitched to two oxen, they drag everything out of the village. I had witnessed that scene several times.

I took my coat off and immediately felt the cold on my back. The winter comes early here. At the end of November snow already falls and covers the peaks with white. The whiteness turns yellow, and remains that way until March.

"Good evening," one of the old men greeted me.

"A good evening to you," I answered in the local dialect.

"This year winter is early, and the cold penetrates right to the bones. When I was young I liked the snow, but now it's my bitter enemy." He spoke as if to an old acquaintance, letting me share his mood.

"It's not forever," I said, glad that I had found the right words.

"It's a frost that won't let up," said the old man emphatically. "Frost like this doesn't pass. It just digs in."

"Does it damage the trees?" I asked for some reason.

"Not necessarily. The trees need a dose of cold, it strengthens them. The summer fruit will be as sweet as honey."

"Thanks." I turned to leave him.

The old man wanted to continue the conversation, but seeing that I had turned aside, he pointed with his cane as if at some distant spot. "A tavern once stood there, and they served French cognac."

The sun dimmed, and evening fell, dressed in violet light. From the low houses scattered along the crests thin smoke rose, reminding me of the days when my parents were alive, and I was shuttled back and forth between them like a defenseless animal. When I was under my father's care, I was entirely his, and even when I wasn't, I wanted to be with him. But recently I have felt my mother's muteness more and more. Sometimes it seems that her despair was refined into a new faith. Father was more practical. He bound his faith together with his practicality, and until his last day he refused to untie the package. Years had passed, but still it was as if we had never parted.

I advanced, now very close to Nachtigel's house. The house lay at the foot of a mountain, surrounded by a snow-covered yard. It looked ordinary, not conspicuous or threatening. Thus, in truth, are all the houses in this area.

Meanwhile, I saw a woman walking down the hill, headed toward the center of the village. She was a short woman of about forty, wearing a knitted hat and a coat like the ones the women of Czernowitz wore before the war.

"Excuse me," I called to her. "Where is Mr. Nachtigel's house?"

"Perhaps you mean the new tenant? It's right in front of you."

"Thank you," I said without moving from the spot. The sky was darkening, and lamps were lit in the houses. The forest all around was thick; I could easily find cover and a vantage point. But for some reason, I stood transfixed by the sight of the evening. It reminded me of another evening, in the forest near Czernowitz. I was four, my mother held my hand, and we made our way through the tall grass. The next day I was going to have my tonsils out, and of course I was afraid. Mother promised me that it was a simple operation and that I wouldn't feel it at all. When I kept asking her how they would remove the infected tonsils, she answered me, in a tone I never heard again from her, "Easily, the way you take a pit from a plum." That voice and the evening mingled together and charmed me, banishing fear from my heart. I returned home happy, drank chocolate, and repeated out loud what my mother had said. "Easily, the way you take a pit from a plum." Later I heard that she was sorry for that little lie.

CHAPTER
28

Now it was completely dark. The few soft lights that shone
in the windows only intensified the darkness all around.
I felt the cold beneath my feet, but knew that I could stand
it for many hours. Since my youth and my travels with
Father, the cold has accompanied me. Sometimes it has
hurt me, but it never killed me the way it killed so many
in the labor camp.

Again I remembered the legless buffet owner, his thin, determined face, the German he spoke. He didn't talk like one of the locals, but in the dialect of the small towns of Austria, where the accent is strong and slightly artificial. Unlike me, he spoke fluently, clearly, with no impediments. I regretted my stammer, the ill-chosen words, the stupid repetitions, and mainly that I left the train quickly, as if fleeing. I ought to have punished the mouth that had uttered the words "a great mission," but I was paralyzed, confused, and without resolve.

In Nachtigel's house no light was lit. I felt that the dread that had oppressed me during the past weeks had subsided inside me. As in the days of my youth, I was prepared to suffer, but I didn't know what the nature of the suffering was to be. For some reason I saw myself running for my life, seeking shelter like my father in the houses of peasants.

To avoid suspicion I went down and strolled along the river. At one time, in moments of exaltation, usually after two or three drinks, agent Murtschik used to talk about the Jews' duty to execute the murderers and to purge the world of its sins. Once he even told me that a religious man was obliged to carry out the sentence—for had the Jews not brought the religion of truth into the world? Those sayings, which he would repeat in many languages, sounded inflated and unpleasant to me. Besides, I suspected he was trying to flatter me so I would pay him more.

Time moved lazily. The center of the village shut down, and only the tavern remained open. The roads were empty, and the few who climbed the hill were middle-aged men who headed straight for the tavern. I, too, wanted to go up and sip a drink. A drink always dissipates fear and gives strength, but I restrained myself and remained at my post.

Last year, at this season, I stayed in a pension for a few days, not far from Weinberg. Hunting down Nachtigel then seemed like a distant wish, as if it belonged more to my old age than to my present. I slept for whole days, immersed in childhood memories and glad for the small amount of cash I had added to my savings. But when I headed south, I knew that if I returned here, it would be different. Then, of course, I didn't imagine that Nachtigel would decide to come out of hiding and buy a house in the area. The moment I learned he was walking about freely, it was clear that I couldn't escape my duty.

At one time I wanted to consult with Rabbi Zimmel about the matter, but in his last years, Rabbi Zimmel was so immersed in preserving his books that I didn't dare impose that burden on him. As I said, just before his death, I told my secret to him. The very act of consultation, it seems to me, is a kind of sharing of the burden.

That's why I didn't consult Max. A person must take an action like this of his own accord.

Strange, I had actually hinted to Bertha that I intended to take Nachtigel's life. The hint was vague, and she didn't catch it. There was a practical reason: I wanted to leave her my small amount of cash, the bankbooks, and a few pictures from home. Someone who sets out on a mission like this has to take into account that he might be wounded or may even die. I was sorry for a moment that the little property I had accumulated over the years would be deposited in a local police station after my death. There they would sort every item, and finally they would burn the clothing, as is the practice here. I wanted to write a note: the cash and the contents of the suitcase, the savings in the bank account in Sandberg, belong to Bertha Kranz. She would certainly report to a police station. As for Nachtigel's death, all the responsibility would be mine. I wanted to write all that, but immediately grasped the foolishness of it.

Gradually, the lights in the houses went out, and only the tavern remained lit. The sounds grew muffled, and were it not for a few birds of prey that sawed the air with their screeches, you could cut the silence into squares.

The cold had seeped into my toes and was now climbing higher. I wasn't tired or faint. My senses were alert and my memory was clear. Still, it seemed to me that those shadows that had followed me over the years, disturbing my sleep and hampering my steps, those malign shadows had finally managed to push me into this trap. Old fears, fears that I had overcome, returned and made my body tremble. Stamping both feet hard, I marched in place. That brief stamping drove away the fear.

Later I thought only of Max, about our friendship and the closeness I feel to him. I wanted to remember how and when I had first met him, but I could not. That practical man, who started with nothing, had taken care of dozens of people. He kept extensive financial records. He was connected with banks and finance companies. He helped people in secret and watched over Rabbi Zimmel. Max, that marvelous man, had been gripped by dread all these years. Sometimes it seemed that he led his life according to signs that he received from distant places. They, in truth, were what guided his life.

Now the feeling grew in me that Max, too, was in danger. I remembered that he had several protected rooms, and not a few pistols. But somehow it seemed to me that he had been trapped in the open store. The cashiers wanted to sound the alarm, but they didn't have time. "May God help him!" I shouted, and I emerged from my waking nightmare.

CHAPTER

29

For hours I stood there. When I awoke the cold had already gripped my whole body. I was surprised at myself for surrendering so easily to my mood. I remembered that one thought had bothered me, gnawed at me all night, and finally it had touched a painful nerve. But what that thought had been, and where it was going, I didn't know. The cold permeated my entire body, and I tried to overcome it.

THE IRON TRACKS

The morning began to glimmer, and the barking of the dogs ceased. Clumps of darkness fell away from the trees. The pain spread through my body. I had known similar pain in my youth, and I was pleased that I had succeeded in standing watch all night without falling asleep.

As the light grew brighter, I saw a man approaching me. He was walking slowly, with a pouch hanging from his shoulder, and he leaned on a cane. He looked like a milkman who had gotten up early, but because he was empty-handed, I changed my mind and imagined he was delivering newspapers. He had an old man's gait, short of breath, stopping every few steps. When he came closer I saw that the pouch wasn't full, but it was still hard for him to carry. His body slouched forward, he was bent over. He seemed to be headed for the commercial center, but to my surprise he turned toward Nachtigel's house.

Without delay I approached him. "Good morning, Colonel Nachtigel."

"A fine morning to you," he replied, revealing a toothless mouth.

"In the name of the neighborhood, I am pleased to greet you."

"Thank you."

"We are very proud of you." The words came to me as if I had rehearsed them.

"It's hard for me to walk." He opened his mouth and gasped for breath.

"But you march like a veteran soldier."

The old man grinned, looked at me in embarrassment, and asked, "Where can you buy milk around here?"

"In the grocery store up there. That's where you'll find all the dairy products, sir." I tried to sound like a local.

"Everything has changed here."

"How so, sir?"

"This whole area used to be part of my father's estate. My elder brother, may he rest in peace, was a wastrel and sold the estate for a pittance. I was in the war and couldn't oversee the family business."

"Here, sir, your service is remembered with pride."

"Never mind," he said, making a dismissive motion and swallowing.

"When do you plan to move in, sir?"

"Soon. For the moment I'm living with my cousin Fritz. He's eight years older than I, and it's very hard for him to walk in the morning."

"But you walk well, sir."

"Not as I once did," he said, and some of his former vigor returned to his face. He leaned on his cane as if he were about to march on, but he changed his mind and added, "It's hard for an old body to endure this cold."

"That's a nice house."

"Since my wife died, life has lost its meaning."

"You mustn't step out of harness," I said, as they do here.

"That's right. But there are days when one has no more will."

"That doesn't apply to old soldiers."

"An old soldier is also a person, isn't he? He also gets old, and he's also miserable." He smiled, and quickly added, "All these years I wanted to return to my childhood home. I was sure that we'd spend our last days together here. But my wife went too soon and left me alone. What's the point of a new house if you haven't anyone to talk to? The walls can drive a man out of his mind."

"Colonel Nachtigel, your former soldiers will come to visit you."

"Today people even forget their fathers and mothers."

"But not their commanders."

He had apparently not expected a compliment like that. He gave me a sad look and said, "So be it." At that moment it was hard to imagine that this man had once worn a uniform, shouted orders, abused people, and shot them the way you shoot stray dogs. He was completely crushed by his misery, and it was clear that no compliment could rouse him from his depression.

"How many years have you lived here?" he asked.

"Many years."

"To my regret, I was distant, though it wasn't my fault, from this place." The slight twists in that sentence showed that the man still hadn't set his thoughts free.

"This land is dear to us all," I said, trying to get him to be sentimental.

"Sir," he replied, raising his eyes, "these places are the true Austria. The rest has already been spoiled."

"True."

"As we used to say in high school, a sound mind in a sound body, isn't it so?" He chuckled, the laugh of an old man whose memory is weak and who is glad of any detail he remembers.

I was shocked at my composure, but still I didn't let up. "Not everything succeeded," I said. "But we didn't lose the war."

"I share your opinion."

"Why, then, this defeatism?"

"From America. All bad things come from America. All the refuse of the world is piled up there, and all the sick ideas come from there." These few words made him stand straighter, and one saw immediately that the man had served in the army from his youth.

"I need milk," he said. "Where's that grocery store?"

"Straight up the hill."

"Once people had dairies and cows. Today every-thing's in a carton." He raised his hand to wave goodbye.

Had it not been for that gesture, it is doubtful that I would have struck at him. But that gesture, more than anything he had said, reminded me of Nachtigel's com-radeship with his young subordinates in the camp, and the warm paternal care he used to shower on them. He treated them like a father, and within a short time he made them as cruel as he was.

The old man walked away, and I opened the valise. I took out the pistol and aimed it straight at his back. The first shot hit him, but he didn't collapse. The second shot knocked him over, and he fell with his arms out-stretched. I wrapped the pistol up again and replaced it in the valise. With quick steps I cleared out.

I knew the forest well, from the times when I used to take the shortcut between Steinberg and Weinberg. The morning light was bright and full, and not a shout or siren could be heard from the main road. I made my way without effort. My arms and legs acted of one accord, but my head was empty, as after a night of drinking.

CHAPTER

3o

I reached the station on time. The express will stop only
in distant Salzstein. But the farther away, the better for
me. Cold morning lights filled the square. People were
buying tickets at the booth. They seemed relaxed. I too
was unafraid. I bought a ticket and boarded the train. It
was warm in the dining car, and the waiter served coffee
and toast.

THE IRON TRACKS

Weinberg used to be one of the last stations on my journey. Here I would burrow into an old pension and sleep for days on end. Five years ago they started holding wild parties in the pensions, or, as they're called here, memorial balls. People would get drunk, sing, and revive memories of their youth and the war. I couldn't bear that sickening sentimentality, and I would head south. My disgust was stronger than my sense of duty. Only later did I learn that Nachtigel was wandering about the region, and I forced myself to stay.

Once I returned to Stark in the middle of the winter. He was very glad to see me, and for a few nights we sat together and read *The Kuzari*. He read with enthusiasm, explicating and arguing from many sources. You could tell that the man was no longer of this world, that he had only returned to it by mistake.

Now that episode, too, was over. Of course, I had imagined the murder differently. I was certain that right afterward I would be killed or at least wounded. Angry people would drag me the length of the streets and slowly, slowly the blood would drip out of my body. The fact that I was alive, sitting on a train and spreading butter on toast, gave me a strange assurance. My anxieties had been in vain, and in a few hours the nightmare would be over. I could return to my usual ways and my regular schedule. The thought that in a few hours the train would

stop in Salzstein erased the sights of the morning from
my eyes and brought me memories from a time when
people from all over would gather in Stark's hut, and
Yiddish was heard among the trees as once it was in cities inhabited by the Jews. For a moment it seemed that
Stark, too, had come back to life, that he was standing
at the door and greeting the people with a beaming smile.
If Stark was alive, then everyone was alive. Gizi, too. A
sandwich was surely waiting for me. One doesn't easily
forget Gizi's thin sandwiches.

I drank three cups of coffee. The liquid seeped
into my limbs, and the cold that had barricaded itself inside my body faded. The cold morning light remained
outdoors. Only the warmth of the sun penetrated the
coach.

While I was sitting and marveling over the annual
cycle, which had suddenly reached its end, a short man
dressed in a long coat approached me. He said in our
language, "You certainly remember me." I saw with dis-
pleasure that he was one of my rivals.

"Where have we met?" I asked.

He named the places, but I did not remember.

"All these years I've wanted to learn from you, but
I didn't succeed. You always got there first. I've decided
to leave, to move to Israel. I won't deny it, I'm leaving
because I have no choice. The chances of making a living
have completely petered out. There's animosity toward

me on the trains. It's better to be among unpleasant Jews than among anti-Semites."

"Is it hard for you to leave?"

"I have no stake here. Except for this route, which I take once or twice a year, I have nothing. Still, it's hard for me to leave that nothing." He chuckled, the laughter of an injured man. "Traveling was once hard for me. Now it's hard for me to do without it."

"Have you wanted to move to Israel for a long time?"

"I'll tell you the truth: I never thought of moving to Israel. The thought of all those Jews crowded in one place depresses me, afflicts me, but what can I do, where shall I go? Necessity cannot be condemned, as they used to say. Did they also say this by you?"

The man's appearance was wretched, and a stench rose from his words as well. But at that moment he was, for some reason, like a brother to me, one whom I had not seen for years. I am your brother, who suddenly appeared and said, don't estrange yourself from me.

"It's good to see you," I said.

"You can be proud of what you have done." He raised his voice. "Not everyone manages to do what you've done."

"What have I done?" I was startled.

"What do you mean? You've discovered all the Jewish antiquities, manuscripts, books. Everything that was buried for years in cellars and attics you've brought out into the daylight. The Jewish people won't forget your contribution."

"I sold it all."

"I used to sell, too. The only difference was, I didn't have anything to sell. I just found leftovers, ordinary things. You found the essential things. Your discoveries are all safe with Max, and when the time comes, they'll be gathered into the treasury of the Jewish people. The Jewish people aren't dust. They're the people of the book who fight for their values."

The more he talked, the more his misery was evident. I wanted to shout, Be quiet. Stop making so much noise. Your words sicken me. You're an empty vessel, not a human being. He must have felt the anger raging within me. Without a word, he stepped aside and vanished from my sight toward the next car. Exhausted, I fell into a deep sleep.

CHAPTER

31

I slept for many hours. When I woke up, the sun had already set, and the train had increased its speed. At first I
imagined that I was headed for Weinberg, but I immediately saw that this wasn't the roomy train that brings va-
cationers to the pensions and ski resorts, but a regular
express returning workers from the north to their homes
and to the long winter idleness. The dining car was full.

People were drinking, chatting, and cursing their bosses and their well-known companies.

Why, then, am I going in the wrong direction? I ask myself. Now I imagined that I had forgotten a package of manuscripts in Gruenwald, one that I had acquired with great difficulty and was about to sell to Max. But a woman, not particularly pretty, had lured me to one of the pensions. In my confusion, I had left that important package in the buffet. I tried to console myself by saying that the buffet owner couldn't read Hebrew, and anyway he wouldn't understand the importance of the find. Then for some reason I remembered my rival and his misery. I couldn't remember what he said to me, but I imagined that he returned to my car and leveled a grave accusation against me, cursing me and threatening to inform on me. Anger that I had suppressed for many days rose up and flooded me. I vowed that if I met him again, I wouldn't spare him, I'd shut his mouth for him.

Fortunately, the express stopped. I saw the familiar Salzstein sign and the platform, and felt relief, as if I had come out of a dark, narrow tunnel that was pressing in on me. I'm back, I said to myself. It was the familiar open area, and if the cold hadn't hit my face, I would have stayed and checked to see if the others had also returned. But the cold was fierce. It drove me into the station and from there to the buffet.

Without doubt this was the beloved Salzstein station, but without Gizi's buffet. To my question, "Where's Gizi?" the buffet owner went straight to the point. "There's no Gizi, no Shmizi. I and no other own the buffet." I said to him, not very cleverly, that every year I return here for a brief gathering, and that we all liked to sit in Gizi's buffet because it was so cozy.

"I threw all that furniture in the garbage. A buffet has to be clean and efficient." So it was: a few plastic tables and chairs, a poster advertising a local band, a jukebox that, for a coin, would play twenty minutes of loud music.

"Sorry," I said and started to leave.

"The man you were speaking of gave lousy service. For thirty years he cheated people."

"He never cheated me." I didn't hold back.

"Maybe. But I wouldn't eat from his loaf."

It hurt me that Gizi, in whose company I had spent many hours every year, that man who had tried to reproduce his lost home in the station, had been ousted. I knew that his wife had waged a massive battle against him. Through her lawyers she had written him threatening letters and filed suit against him. But I never thought he would end up destitute. Where is he, that dear man, I wanted to ask. But I knew that there was no one to answer.

I went outside. I had stood in this place a few months ago and said goodbye to Stark. His look had been full of meaning, and he had stood there and marvelled at everything that took place on this earth. I knew that he had taken leave of me, but I refused to accept his farewell. His mind hadn't gone soft like some of the others. He had simply returned to his ancestors and their books, finding there what he hadn't found in his youth.

I walked up to his cabin. Unlike in the summer, the heights were exposed, and I could see the many fields and the orchards. I remembered the singing and the lofty speeches about recovery and reorganization, and a special program to help the scattered few out of their despair and mourning. I remembered the plan to establish a publishing house and a new journal. Above all, I remembered the ceaseless war against melancholy.

When I reached Stark's cabin, a young nun greeted me. She told me that the old man had gone to his eternal rest, and that the local council had transferred his house to the church. Now it served as a chapel for wayfarers.

"And the books and journals?" I asked apprehensively.

In response to my question, the nun opened the cabin door, to reveal an astonishing sight. The books, newspapers, magazines, and pamphlets that had been scattered all those years on chairs, dresser, and floor were now arranged on new shelves. The evening light illuminated the empty space and a lucid serenity, found only in places devoid of people, pervaded the room.

"And what will become of these books?"

"They are here," said the nun. "Whoever wants to consult them can do so." Her face was young and round and flushed, suffused with a strange innocence. I bowed my head as if my shame were revealed.

I turned aside and went out to circle the plateau. In the past we used to come out in twos and threes, sometimes five of us, to circle it. That was part of the ritual, one of the things we would do during the sleepless nights we spent at Stark's. At dawn we would return and sing, "The Jewish people live, the Jewish people live." Some comrades objected to it, arguing that Bnei Akiva, the religious youth movement, used to sing it before the war. But Stark approved of it. His argument was that now we had to fortify ourselves, and that whatever supported the sanctuary of life and inspired hope was permitted.

Afterward we would drink coffee, and the debates were bitter. Old words and new ones would be woven together into a prolonged roar. Stark would produce arguments from Midrashim and from famous Hasidic works. Some comrades would dismiss them, saying you can't bring evidence from decaying books. Others wept in despair, as if the yawning abyss had just been revealed before their eyes. In the afternoon sleep would descend on everyone. Stark would sit at his desk and write letters to close friends and to friends who had abandoned him.

CHAPTER

32

When I reached the station it was already night. Once I
knew the train schedule by heart. Now the connections
seemed all wrong. I had forgotten: this wasn't my usual
place in this season. The winter schedule is different
from the spring.

"I have to get to Wirblbahn urgently." I addressed
the cashier, my voice slightly raised.

"If so, don't skimp, sir. Buy an express ticket. The express will arrive in one hour." She spoke like one of the peasants who crowded around the ticket booth. Her direct, businesslike approach, which was meant only to be helpful, aroused a repressed fear in me.

"I wouldn't want to arrive in the middle of the night," I said.

"No," said the cashier. "You'll arrive in daylight."

"Many thanks," I said, embarrassed that I had revealed my fears.

I thought of Gizi and stayed out of the buffet. Standing in the plaza, I was surrounded by memories from the past. For many years this had been my life's meeting place. From here I would embark on my journeys, taking the memory of my parents with me to every station. Once in a remote pension, one of Stark's faithful had said to me in an anxious voice, full of fear, "I'm afraid to go up to Stark's now. His soul has been reborn in another soul. He's no longer the Communist I once knew."

"He's returned to his ancestors," I tried to convince him. But he wouldn't accept that. He kept arguing that a frightening change had taken place in Stark, and that people should stay away from his cabin. Otherwise he would infect them with his strange thoughts. Now, as if in a dream, I remembered the man, the way he stood and his frightened look.

An elderly traveler turned to me. "Where are you going, if I may ask?"

"To Wirblbahn."

"My God," said the man. "That's a desolate place."

"Not for me," I answered.

"During the war I guarded the warehouse there," the man confessed.

"The place is going to change very soon," I told him.

"The ones with physical limitations were sent there."

"What was that like?"

"Disgusting."

"Why?"

"Because the men my age were at the front. They fought and were wounded and died like heroes. And I was sorting equipment, whitewashing paths, polishing shoes, and at night, guarding the warehouses." The man was about seventy, and it was clear that that distant, shameful memory still lodged in his heart.

"Everyone had his own war," I said.

"It was all because of a limp. An almost unnoticeable one. After the war the soldiers returned from the front and told of signs and wonders, and you were the fool of the family. You sat in the corner, mute as a stone."

"But a lot of them died." I tried to console him.

"To me in those years, death was preferable to service in Wirblbahn. Now I'm an old man." He gestured in a way that reminded me, sharply, of the gesture that Nachtigel made before I killed him, a gesture that said, My life has passed me by, and there's no point in changing it.

I observed him again. He was slightly stooped, leaning on his cane, and it was clear that his life had not gone well. Now, approaching its end, it had become loathsome.

"If they had sent me to the front, my life would have been entirely different," he said in a trembling voice.

"How so?"

"In every way. I would have been a different man. I would have married a different woman. I would have had different children. There would have been light in my life."

The train arrived and our conversation was cut short. I hurriedly boarded one of the rear cars. It was a new train, open, the kind you don't see in the provinces. A smell of fresh sawdust filled the air.

The old man got on and sat down beside me. He continued talking about that disgrace known as Wirblbahn, which had blackened and disfigured his life. In the end he had had to make a living from what his ancestors had bequeathed to him, a wretched living.

Later we sat in the dining car, and I offered him a drink. The drink also failed to banish the shame from his memory. Indeed it seemed to intensify it. He blamed his father, who had neglected to have his leg treated. Instead of sending him to Vienna he had scraped together pennies to give his daughter a decent dowry.

"And what will you do in Wirblbahn, sir?" he asked me.

"I intend to burn Wirblbahn down," I said clearly.

"How?" said the old man in a coarse voice, exposing what remained of his teeth.

"Just as I said."

"Are you an engineer, sir?"

"Yes, sir."

"That idea never occurred to me at all."

"It's a dreadful place and it has to be destroyed. I'll do it with a clear mind and without any pangs of conscience. You must not leave such places in the world."

"You're right. And what are they planning build there?"

"I don't know yet. First, the place has to be razed to the ground. Only then can we see what's to be done."

"That's a wise step," said the old man, and in his dulled eyes the painful memory was lit up once more. "It's a shame I wasted my youth there."

"Don't worry. We won't leave a trace."

"When are you going to do it?"

"In the next few days. That's why I'm going there."

The Iron Tracks

"You're doing a good thing, sir," the old man mumbled, and his head sank wearily onto the table.

I, too, was tired. My words weakened me and made me dizzy. Yellow flames writhed before my eyes, mingling with black flames. It was clear that my life in this place had burned up and come to an end. If I had a different life, it wouldn't be happy. As in all my clear and drawn-out nightmares, I saw the sea of darkness, and I knew that my deeds had neither dedication nor beauty. I had done everything out of compulsion, clumsily, and always too late.

Aharon Appelfeld was nine when he witnessed the murder of his mother by the Nazis. After escaping from a concentration camp, he wandered in the forests for two years. When the war ended he joined the Soviet Army as a kitchen boy, eventually emigrating to Palestine in 1946. The author of twelve internationally acclaimed novels, including *Badenheim 1939, The Conversion, The Age of Wonders, Tzili, To the Land of the Cattails,* and *Katerina,* he lives in Jerusalem.

THE PERIODIC TABLE by Primo Levi
0-8052-1041-5

THE SCHOCKEN BOOK OF CONTEMPORARY
JEWISH FICTION
Edited by Ted Solotaroff and Nessa Rapoport
0-8052-1065-2

THE FORGOTTEN by Elie Wiesel
0-8052-1019-9

Available at your local bookstore,
or call toll-free: 1-800-733-3000 (credit cards only).

Printed in the United States
by Baker & Taylor Publisher Services